TEDDY WAINWRIGHT

AND THE CASE OF THE

MURDERED MOVIE MOGUL

A CELLULOID DETECTIVE MYSTERY

JULIE B. BRAYTON

Teddy Wainwright & the Case of the Murdered Movie Mogul
by Julie B. Brayton
Copyright © 2014 Julie B. Brayton

Editing & formatting by Clare C. Marshall
Cover design by David Farrell

This book is dedicated to my wonderful parents who have always encouraged me. This is for them.

CHAPTER ONE

The chain around my waist was cutting off all my air.

I gasped, trying to pull in enough of the sweet, lifesaving oxygen but it was oh, so difficult. I could no longer focus on the mission that had brought me to Montgomery's office. My face was probably a kaleidoscope, cycling through various colors. It would start with purple, and then blossom into an alarming shade of red, before finally ending with a pasty white as my lifeless, airless body, collapsed into a pitiful, yet artistic, heap on the floor—

Hold it!

Drat it all, my imagination was running away with me again. Everyone had their share of bad habits. One of my worst was letting my mind whirl around unchecked. Left to its own devices it was able to conjure up all sorts of scenarios, each more absurd than the last. I always had an active imagination, ever since I toddled out of the nursery. It evolved from a necessity to escape the extreme boredom inflicted by being in the presence of my family. As I'd sat ram-rod straight on the hard, wooden chair in my mother's sun porch, I conjured up wild adventures in my mind. I would explore the darkest jungle, uncover the greatest of archaeological treasures, and scale the highest mountain, all while displaying an excellent example of a prim and proper boy. I should've won an Academy Award back then for Best Actor in the role *Appearing Interested When He Really Wasn't,* but I digress.

My crazy imagination was a trait I had to forcefully shut down on the battlefields of France to survive the Great War. Conjuring up creative ways to risk life and limb hadn't been nearly as much fun when the reality of death was so vividly on display before my eyes. Still, even after spending a horrendous six months in the trenches, I had survived. It turned out my ability to create innovative scenarios out of thin air actually helped get me out of those trenches, but that is neither here nor there. Sometimes it was fun, following the bizarre paths my mind would lead me, but other times it wasn't so helpful.

Take the current situation. Was my doom really as impending as it seemed at first? I risked another cautious breath. Yes the chain—all right, elastic waistband if you insist on accuracy—kept my midsection from expanding to full capacity. My imminent demise due to oxygen starvation was apparently not so imminent after all. I had triumphed over the situation. I was in command. I was a man of action. A daring man who had not only survived the Great War, but solved at least twelve of the most heinous crimes ever thought up by man, or at least one very determined woman. I could do this. I would do this.

Buoyed by my determination, I slipped my hand beneath my waistband and tugged at my girdle. Blast it! How in the world did women wear these things every day?

I pulled until the elastic loosened just a fraction of an inch, letting my manly chest catch a full breath while smothered inside a decidedly female torture implement. The tingling in my midsection eased just a bit. I was still uncomfortable, but at least the threat of immediate death seemed to be diverted, at least for the moment.

My body was rather fetching in its natural male form, or so I've been told. I topped close to six feet, had brown hair tinged with black, and if I looked closely the occasional streak of gray, I chose not to look closely. I also was blessed with brown eyes and rather chiseled features. Attributes that were an enhancement on the silver screen, however they did not look nearly so fetching while ensconced in a decidedly female outfit. Fortunately good looks were not required for this particular assignment.

Once again fortified with some of that really good Hollywood air, I felt ready to jump back into battle once again. I raised my weapon and began my attack.

Flicking the feather duster back and forth, I made sure to brush against every nook and cranny, groove and surface of the statues and awards ever so neatly arrayed on the bookshelf. No dirt spores were going to get away while I was on the job. However, it wasn't easy, keeping this office that was a tribute to art deco tidy. The velvet material covering the plush sitting chairs seemed to attract dust like nothing else, as did the bookshelves and end tables made from the finest mahogany wood. Even the expensive globe, resting on its very own stand nestled in the corner, wasn't immune to a dusty assault.

Still, I wasn't going to give up. While I worked to turn the room into a model of cleanliness, which could proudly be featured in any architectural magazine, I thought about my own apartment, the one Sally gleefully referred to as "The Garbage Dump." Here I was frantically cleaning someone else's office, while I let my own living space degrade into piles of dust and junk. I thought about it as I switched out the feathers for a soft cloth and attacked the coffee rings left on top of an end table. The conclusion I came up with was simple.

Cleaning up at home was work. This was suffering for my art.

I suspected Sally would not be impressed with this argument. More likely she would laugh at me, and then ring up several of our mutual friends to make sure they would all have a snicker or two at my expense. No matter, if a little cleaning could help me become a better actor, so be it. I soldiered on.

A rustle of movement captured my attention. I had been so lost in my thoughts I had totally forgotten I was the interloper here. The rightful occupant of this office—R.K. Montgomery—was indeed present and sitting restlessly in his chair. He was focused solely on the script in his hand.

I wondered if I should speak to him. Offer to refill the coffee which was slowly cooling on his desk. Go to the commissary to fetch a sandwich, even though it would close in a few minutes. The commissary was only open for breakfast and lunch, leaving anyone who worked the night shift on their own and out of luck if they happened to be working after hours. It was a travesty I was going to bring up to the head of the studio when I had time—

Wait, the time could be now. I was standing right behind him! I could speak out and demand change, if I was here as Theodore Wainwright, actor extraordinaire and star of the most successful movie series on the lot, but I wasn't here as an actor. At the moment I wasn't a movie star at all. I was a cleaning lady. One to be seen, not heard, and certainly not one to fetch food. I was here to clean, not to become a common waitress.

Focusing on my work, I moved on from the table, and paid careful attention to the cabinet containing an expensive radio set, working hard to polish the surface to a fine shine. Was my act convincing? Another glance found that Montgomery was totally oblivious to my presence. A good thing, I supposed.

A squeak of wheels shattered the silence. I risked a glance toward the desk. Reading time was over, apparently. The script was laying the great man's lap, and he was pulling a cart closer to his deck. On the cart was a giant recording device businessman used to record letters or instructions for their secretaries to transcribe later. While it was the latest technology, it must have weighed fifty pounds, easy.

I compared it to the giant sound equipment they trundled onto the set when I shot my first talking motion picture. All of the machinery needed to preserve my voice for posterity took up half a room. The microphone they slid under my ass and then taped to my chest was the size of a discus. Hiding it was no easy feat, let me tell you.

The recording device by the desk was the size of three bread boxes stacked on top of one another. I knew from previous experience with such units that the case housed a giant cylinder that, when spinning, recorded sound so it could be played back later.

It was a bit of a miracle if one thought about it, but then so were motion pictures. They were my own personal miracle. Without movies I would probably be dead, or even worse, trapped on that Palm Beach estate watching my mother looking down her nose at her lessors. I stifled a shudder. It was a fate too horrible to contemplate.

Montgomery flipped the switch and a hum filled the room as the cylinders spun up to full speed. He reached for the microphone with an ease born of practice, and then R.K. Montgomery, head of one of the biggest movie studios in Hollywood, began to speak. "Mrs. Rivers, take a letter," he said into the recording machine. "To Laszlo Farnsworth, head of the Motion Picture Production Code."

The Motion Picture Production Code? I was too far away make out the words written on the script resting on Montgomery's lap, but I could see some of the passages had been marked up by a red pen. Red for changes? Were those changes the work of the decency code?

"Dear Laszlo," Montgomery said. "I thank you for your call of the nineteenth, and for sending over your suggestions for improving some of our latest productions." Montgomery plucked the script gingerly from his lap. He held it by two fingers only, as if the paper was contaminated by some dreadful disease, and then dangled it over the waste basket. With great deliberation, Montgomery parted his fingers. The script slid from his hand, landing in the trash with a plop.

So much for the suggestions from the Production Code.

"I know as the self-appointed Paragon of Virtue, you believe you know what is best for all of us when it comes to writing and producing films. I appreciate your intention to ensure that the highest moral values are included in each and every movie made, but I'm afraid, dear Laszlo, the films produced here at RKM Studios will have to muddle through without your input for the foreseeable future. Continued good health, to you and yours. Sincerely, R.K. Montgomery." Montgomery turned off the noisy machine, and a blessed silence descended upon the room.

I was so caught up in seeing a glimpse of a movie mogul in action that I forgot I was supposed to be working. Deciding the feather duster hadn't removed enough dust spores, I abandoned the coffee rings and started polishing one of Montgomery's Oscars with my soft cloth.

"You'll wear off the gold plate Teddy, if you keep rubbing that so hard."

Drat it, caught in the act. I lowered my polishing cloth. "How did you know, R.K.?"

"Like I wouldn't recognize my biggest star the moment he stepped into the room."

"That's no explanation." I gestured toward my lovely outfit. "Look at me. My disguise is perfect."

"It is pretty good," Montgomery agreed, before getting up and moving toward the globe. He ran his fingers across the smooth, polished surface, and unlatched a nearly invisible small clasp tucked away in the molding. "Nice cleaning job, by the way."

"Ha."

Smiling at his own wit, Montgomery flipped open the top half of the world, revealing a hidden mini bar inside. I hadn't been expecting that. "Impressive."

"It helps the image when I have visitors of, shall we say, a more conservative nature."

"Like Farnsworth?"

"Like Farnsworth." Montgomery cracked the cap off of a very nice and very expensive bottle of Scotch. "Your imper-sonation was nearly perfect."

"Nearly? That's a bunch of crap. My disguise is perfect, and you know it." I'd spent several days making damn sure it would be. First I studied the women who cleaned after hours as they went about their business. Most of them were European, and had escaped to the New World following the Great War, no doubt. Some were young, but a few were graying, and I copied the exact gray hue onto my wig. They all wore the same drab brown blouse and skirt, with a matching kerchief to hold their hair out of their eyes. It was the very same outfit I was now ensconced in, to my great discomfort. I had purloined, or that is to say, *borrowed*, from the ladies changing room earlier in the week. I also borrowed a cart full of every cleaning implement ever imagined by mankind, which was currently sitting outside Montgomery's door. The portable metal shelf was crammed with so many items I could hardly identify half of them, and in one case quite frankly, I wasn't sure if I wanted to know what the hell it was supposed to be used for. Add some glasses to obscure my eyes, and a wart on my cheek for a touch of realism, and voila, one debonair, dashingly handsome, and decidedly male movie star, transformed into middle aged washer-woman. "There's no way you should have recognized me."

Montgomery handed me a glass, then snapped the globe shut. His lips twitched for a few moments, but at least he had the decency not to laugh. "There were two small things that stood out."

"Only two?"

"Don't get huffy, Theodore." Montgomery took a healthy swig of Scotch. "Number one, you were too good at your job."

"Since when is efficiency a liability?"

"It is if you're trying to imitate a woman who only makes two dollars a month. She only cleans twice a week and her skills leave much to be desired." He ran his fingers over the top of the immaculate globe. "You did too good a job."

Drat it again. Sally always told me I thought the best of people, even to my own determent. I always assumed everyone's work ethic was as rigorous as my own. I would have to keep that in mind during my next impersonation. "You said there were two things?"

"I recognized your walk."

"My what?"

"Your feet." He gestured to the floor. "You take an extra half-step sometimes when you walk."

"I do?"

"You're the only person I've ever seen who walks in such a manor. I still don't know how you can keep upright, but you never fall."

I looked down. Now the feet I have always known looked like strange apparitions. Could I possibly ever walk again? Then I tossed all thoughts of shuffling feet aside, as the perfect argument came to me. "Don't you see, RK? You were only able to unmask me because you knew about a personal habit of mine. Otherwise I was the perfect cleaning woman. Too clean in your own words." I set my glass down, careful to put it on a coaster. No point in ruining my hard work. "I know I can become almost anyone. I can become *Theodore Wainwright, Man of a Thousand Disguises*."

"Maybe you can," Montgomery conceded, "but I don't want you too."

"Why?"

"Isn't it obvious, Teddy? People don't want to see this." Montgomery snatched the gray wig and the scarf from my head. "Millions of lovely young ladies all around this fine country of ours think they're in love with Detective Woodrow C. Tompkins. Sure he is a fictional fellow, but they believe in him because of you. Every one of these girls is happy to plunk down a dime or two at their nearby picture palace each and every weekend and why? It's more than simply watching Tompkins catch the bad guy. They long for the chance to drool over your incredibly handsome face."

"But RK—"

"And may I remind you, Mr. Wainwright, that there's a depression raging outside our studio gates. Hundreds of people who work on this lot are not standing in bread lines right now along with a good portion of the American populace, and do you know why?"

I had a sinking feeling I did. "Because of my handsome face?"

"Exactly. All those millions of dimes that the girls keep paying, even in the middle of hard times like these, add up to hundreds of thousands of dollars. Dollars that make the bottom line of this otherwise cash-strapped studio black instead of red. Dollars that mean we are not covering up this." He waved the wig in front of my handsome face. "Now, do you understand?"

"Yes, RK."

"No more talk about becoming the man of a thousand disguises?"

"No, RK."

"Good man." Montgomery set his glass down on the table. I was pleased to see that he used the coaster. The studio head was no dummy. He headed toward his coat rack on the other side of the office and put on his Chesterfield wool overcoat. "I am a late for Gloria Cooper's wrap party. The press will be there so I have to get going. You should get going too. Tomorrow is the final day of shooting for *Detective Tompkins and the Case of the Misfiled Corpse*. We don't want shadows appearing beneath those handsome eyes to ruin RKM's next blockbuster, do we?'

"No, RK." Thoroughly cowed, I began to shuffle out.

"Oh, and Teddy."

"Yes?"

When I turned, he was pointing to the molding on the bookshelf to my right. "You missed a spot."

I barely kept myself from throwing the feather duster at him.

I was about to storm out when Montgomery's office door flew open. The man who entered moved quickly, but I would have recognized those tweed trousers and that tweed jacket anywhere. They belonged to Timothy Edmunds, casting director here at RKM Studios. Timothy stormed toward Montgomery, apparently I wasn't the only one who had perfected the act of storming. He clutched something in his hand. I couldn't quite see what. He moved past me as if I wasn't there, which encouraged me. Timothy saw me fairly often, sometimes every week, yet he didn't instantly recognize me. Perhaps my disguise was better than Montgomery had first thought.

Timothy nearly stepped on the great Montgomery's feet, he had gotten so close. Strange, I had always thought of Timothy as sort of an easy going sort of fellow, yet here he was, waving a piece of paper right in the face of the man who employed us all. "Mr. Montgomery. I searched for weeks to find the perfect actress to play the divorcee in your latest steamy, seductress film. Barbara Sanders can play a femme fatale better than anyone else in town, but now I found out you replaced her behind my back, with a girl barely out of high school. She has neither the skills nor talent to take on such a complex and challenging role, yet you gave it to her. Why?"

Montgomery finished putting on his coat and then reached for his gloves. "If you have noticed her rather ample bosom, then you would know why."

I didn't mean to blush, but I did.

Timothy didn't blush, but he didn't appear to be satisfied either. "You are essentially tossing all hopes of making a profit into the garbage."

"Oh, I don't think so. *The Divorcee* would never be considered a work of fine art in any case, and as we both know, sex sells." Montgomery finished with his gloves, reached for his walking stick, then headed for the door. "Sorry, Timothy, but the change stays." Montgomery stopped in the doorway and looked back at us both. "You gentlemen have a good night now." Montgomery made a predictably dramatic exit, complete with a peal of laughter that echoed far, far down the hallway.

We stood alone in the great man's office, and then Timothy began to mutter. "Pompous old goat. Ruining a perfectly good picture for no reason. Just because of the size of a woman's bust line—" Timothy suddenly stopped and stared my way. "Gentlemen?" He peered at me closely. I held up my feather duster and tried to look as womanly as I could but to no avail. "Theodore, is that you in that dress?"

***

I felt much better, dressed as a man once again.

The transformation came in my private dressing room, but since I was a so-called star, it actually was more private small building than a single room. I had made it all the way from the administration building unseen, or I hoped so anyway. The image of me wearing a dress without a wig would've been something quite spectacular to anyone who happened to pass by. Even more spectacular were the maneuvers I needed to go through to get the damn thing off. If that had been captured on film, it would've been an award-winner all by itself.

I'd been wearing that cursed girdle for only a couple of hours, yet by the time I was done with Montgomery it was practically fused on. Not wanting to waste the garment I struggled in vain for a while, tugging and pulling it dreadfully out of shape. Finally I said to hell with it and attacked it with a pair of sewing shears. Once free of the clingy elastic, I enjoyed breathing freely for a few minutes, and then cheerfully tossed the offending item into the trash. Removing the rest of the cleaning lady attire was easy in comparison.

Now, what to replace it with? Taking the time to inspect the wardrobe choices I had in the closet in my dressing room, I finally selected my finest forty-dollar Herringbone suit. Yes, I know, I spent too much on clothes. The forty-dollars didn't even include the cost of tailoring. I paid extra to garment experts in Beverly Hills to make darn sure the fit was perfect. It was well worth the expense in my mind since there was nary a wrinkle to be found. It was dark brown, which offset my eyes, and it was made of pure wool. The suit coat covered a crisp white shirt and a suit-matching brown waistcoat. I fussed until the tip of one of my handkerchiefs peeked perfectly out of my front pocket. A fedora perched atop my head completed the ensemble and I was ready to be seen in public once again.

I stopped by the ladies changing room in the administration building to quietly return the cleaning outfit I had borrowed. Fortunately no one was around and I slipped in and out unnoticed. I also left a couple of dollars on top of the locker where I had taken the girdle. While the woman who originally owned the garment wouldn't know exactly what the money was for, I hoped she would use it to purchase a replacement.

Next I was off across the lot to the writer's bungalow. There I would find the two females who loved me best. After my less than satisfactory meeting with Montgomery, I needed some cheering up.

Darn that R.K. Ever since he mentioned my half-step, I'd been keeping an eye on my feet to see what they were actually doing, which turned out to be a terrible idea. I mean, who really pays attention to how they walk? The second I tried to puzzle out the mechanics of walking, my legs, perhaps embarrassed by the scrutiny, seem to take on a life of their own.

They moved independently from one another and nearly landed me and my lovely suit on my ass, twice. When I nearly fell for the third time I said to hell with it. I'd been walking just fine with a half-step for thirty-four years now. I wasn't going to worry about it anymore.

My pace and mobility restored, I arrived at my destination without further incident. Upon entering the room I removed my fedora, as any gentleman would, and paused in the doorway. It should have seemed more impressive, this room where cinematic masterpieces like the Tompkins Mystery series were born. Before I came to work here, I always thought the creative center of RKM Studios should be as grand as the sets on the movies themselves. The writer's bungalow should have had walls made of marble, the most expensive of furniture to sit upon, and the finest of art adorning the walls. It should have been a palace to reflect the importance of the location. Instead I was disappointed when all I found was a bunch of rickety desks, complete with even more rickety chairs to support the writers who churned out script after script on typewriters that must have been born closer to the last century, than the current one.

The name on the door pronounced that the RKM's head writer was a man named Harvey Spencer. As far as I was concerned he could have been named Harvey the Ghost. He never seemed to be around, so perhaps he was haunting the place. There was a more substantial, and less interesting reason for his absence. The man was a bit of a lush and was probably sleeping it off in an alley somewhere. Everybody knew about Spencer's drinking problem, but because he had one big hit at the dawn of the talkies he was a name Montgomery could sell to the public. So now he was the head writer, he just didn't do any of the work. Fortunately RKM had a talented staff to pick up the slack.

Since it was past the close of business hours most of the others were gone, but the room wasn't completely empty. Two living, breathing beauties were still there, sharing a desk. They were so cute together I wished I hadn't left my Brownie camera in my dressing room. The taller female sat in the chair, clacking away at the typewriter keys.

When I first encountered Sally Kahili Jones on that beach in Waikiki so many years ago, I could have never imagined how far we would travel together. Our friendship began with her knuckles firmly making contact with my face. Of course I deserved it, daring to steal a kiss at the tender age of ten. She said she had long since forgiven me for my indiscretions, and despite a rocky beginning, we were now the very best of friends.

I knew better than to greet Sally first. If I didn't shower the proper attention onto the other main lady in my life, I would feel the repercussions immediately, and painfully by way of claws digging into my arm. "How is the most beautiful girl in the world?" Sally didn't even look up. Even though she was indeed beautiful. Her light brown hair, quaffed into artificial curls via home permanent, as was all the rage. It compliment-ed her silky skin, white with just a tinge of copper, as if she was always sporting an athletic tan. But Sally knew I wasn't talking about her at the moment. "You are so gorgeous," I crooned, walking up to the desk. "I love you so much." I ran my hands over the silky, smooth fur of the most gorgeous Maine Coon cat I had ever seen, and gently picked her up and cradled her. "Hello my sweet Princess Penelope. Did you miss your daddy?"

"Oh, please," Sally muttered. "You're going to make me nauseous."

I cuddled Penelope even closer to me, and put a protective

hand over her ears. "Don't listen to the mean lady, precious. She's just jealous."

"Ha."

I put my beloved Penelope back on the desk, then went around to give Sally a peck. "I wish I had it as good as your cat," she said, leaning her cheek outward to receive my gesture of affection. She never punched me when I kissed her anymore, well almost never. "Penelope gets to lay around all day, pampered and petted until mealtime. Then for dinner, she gets the best liver in a crystal bowl."

"Silver chalice," I corrected, falling into the seat opposite her. "And I would be happy to pamper you, if you'd let me."

"I'm an independent girl who likes to make her own way, Teddy, as you know perfectly well. You got me this job, that's enough."

"Yes, I know." I had to fight down a smile as I always did when Sally's independent streak appeared. She would think I was laughing at her, yet I was really just enjoying her spirit. She was such a refreshing departure from most women I knew. "Have you heard from your parents lately?"

"A letter from Mother arrived yesterday."

"How are they?" I couldn't read the letter even if Sally offered it to me. I didn't speak or read Hawaiian.

"They're fine. Father's a bit grumpy since his retirement from the army. Mother's trying to get him to join a local group of older Hawaiian warriors to share battle history and stories."

"Really?" I could just picture it. A veteran of the American military, originally from Texas, sitting with a storied Hawaiian warrior over some Mai Tai's, deciding which weapon was better: the machine gun or Hawaiian spears edged with sharks teeth, and all the while, Sally's mother standing smugly in the background. Oh, how I loved Sally's family. They were such a refreshing change from my own.

Paper rustled as Sally straightened the pages of her latest opus, and then she petted Penelope. Not a full-handed stroke, mind you, but a Sally pet consisted of a single forefinger briefly rubbing atop Penelope's skull. See, I knew, deep down, she loved my princess as much as I did. "How did it go with, Mr. Montgomery?" she asked.

I sighed. "I'm too pretty."

"Hmm." She studied me carefully, as if searching for my handsome allure, and had failed to find it. "I take it Mr. Montgomery didn't see any profit in covering up your handsome face?"

"He claimed everyone on the lot would soon be on the breadlines if every single one of my features wasn't fully exposed at all times."

"Well, look at the amount of fan mail you get, Teddy. Mr. Montgomery does have a point."

"Maybe so, but drat it all!" I jumped to my feet, startling Penelope from her latest nap. "I'm so bored with Detective Tompkins. He's always slinking around darkened corners in the dead of night, asking ridiculous questions of suspects. Then he gathers them all together in the parlor to engage in some dreadful exposition—no slight intended to your fabulous writing Sally—before unmasking the killer. It's always the same in every movie. Now you know I can conjure up anyone I want in my mind."

"Yes I know," she said quietly. "It's a trait of yours that saved your life in the war, and I'll be forever grateful for it."

"Me too." At first, the army had thrown me in the trenches like every other doughboy, but after a while, they saw that I had different strengths to offer up for the cause. So began a set of adventures of a more clandestine nature that I was still not at liberty to discuss today. "Back to Detective Tompkins. I know I have the talent and the capability to create any character I want and become anyone I want, yet here I am reciting the same old lines, and repeating essentially the same old story week after week after week, and I'm so dreadfully tired of it."

"So you're stuck?" I nodded. "And you've come to my office to sulk?" Another nod.

Now, it was an established fact that Sally knew me better than I knew myself, but I knew a thing or two about her as well—I could tell she was annoyed with me. Really annoyed. "What?"

"You don't want to give up playing Detective Tompkins altogether, do you?"

"Of course not. Even before Montgomery told me I was the only thing keeping everyone on the lot off the streets, I knew darn well where my personal bread is buttered. I just want to expand my skills, explore new roles. Act in something interesting for a change."

"Even if you don't make a lot of money, or get a lot of credit?"

"Even then."

"Did you share all these personal ambitions with Mr. Montgomery, or did you only threaten to derail his money train?"

I had mentioned all this to Montgomery, hadn't I? "Well—"

"Oh Theodore." She only used my full name when she thought I was a drooling idiot. Perhaps I was.

"He cut me off before I got a chance." Was that a hint of a whine in my tone?

"And then you panicked under the weight of his monetary expectations and you let him scare you away."

I hadn't thought of the encounter in quite so cowardly terms, but of course she was right. "If I had a tail I would have scuttled with it tightly between my legs."

"My dear Teddy. You are so sweet, but sometimes you are so naïve."

I worked to tamp down my temper. While I loved Sally dearly, there were times when she made my blood boil. Times like now, when she was treating me like a five year old. A rather simple five year old. "In what way am I being naïve?"

"Teddy, Mr. Montgomery's continued employment is linked to your success as well. He needs you." If she had clunked me over the head with a plank I couldn't have been more stunned. I was indeed naïve, and an idiot too. That thought had never occurred to me. "The trouble with you, Teddy, is you're far too nice sometimes. You need to stand up to Mr. Montgomery. Threaten him. Make him give you what you want."

"But Sally, I can't leave RKM and put all our friends out of work."

"Of course not, but you don't need to share that particular information with Mr. Montgomery." She smiled at me and pointed toward the door, expecting her order to be obeyed. "You want to expand your acting skills? Well here is your chance. You go back to his office right now and act tough."

"Yes ma'am." Firm, strong and full of determination I got to my feet, ready for action. Then I remembered: "I can't go right now, Mr. Montgomery is gone for the evening. Off to Gloria Cooper's wrap party if I recall correctly."

"Then you'll have to go see him first thing in the morning," she insisted.

"No can-do," I countered. I have to finish up shooting on *Detective Tompkins and the Case of the Misfiled Corpse*. That should take up a good chunk of the day."

"But not all of the day," Sally insisted. "You march right over to his office as soon as you are free from the set tomorrow, and you don't come back until you get Mr. Montgomery to agree to let you play another role."

"Yes ma'am," I fired off a salute her father would be proud of. I had no choice but to obey her. Penelope wasn't the only princess in the room.

***

It wasn't bad being outside in November, with the sun shining bright in sunny Southern California. Or it wouldn't be bad if we didn't add hot giant lights to amp up the total wattage. The amount of light needed to shoot a film had been reduced in recent years as the quality of the black and white film improved, but it was still ridiculously massive. Even in what passes for winter around here, the makeup artist was fighting a losing battle trying to blot away the sweat from my brow. I thanked her for her efforts. It was probably all for the best anyway. I was an artist, and therefore born to suffer.

A small breeze blew by, which raised my spirits. Despite the heat, it was nice to be outside instead of trapped in the drab confines of a soundstage. Today we were shooting the first scene of *Detective Tompkins and the Case of the Misfiled Corpse* at the little park situated at the heart of the RKM backlot. Of course this was happening on the last day of filming, since we completed shooting the rest of the movie earlier. Leave it to the film industry to do everything backwards. Hidden in the insanity of scheduling, there was a method to this madness. Shooting outside was more expensive of course, even if it was on our lot. My favorite director, Douglas Keene, was no dummy. He knew as well as I that everything looked more realistic if it was, in fact, real. Sure, you could recreate a park inside a soundstage, but that would be a last resort. Before we even started shooting a frame of this film, Keene placed this scene last on the shooting schedule. He hoped if he pinched his pennies while shooting the rest of the movie, we would have enough money left over to film this last scene outside, and it worked. Detective Tompkins was able to tail a suspect through actual trees while actual birds were flying and a real breeze was blowing.

It should've been a fitting beginning to a heart-clenching whodunit, but I had to admit I wasn't putting my best effort into the scene. Although I had memorized my lines long ago, my mind was not on my work. I found myself going through the motions, saying the lines that needed to be said. I had played Tompkins for so long, I didn't have to reach too far inside me to find his soul. This left me plenty of cerebral space to think about last night, about Sally and about Montgomery. Did the leader of RKM really need me as much as I needed him?

I wasn't used to being needed, not really. To my mother I was some sort of trophy to show off. To my father I was a rather strange duck, since I had no interest in the family business, but I was a presence he still tolerated from time to time. To my sister I was an annoyance to be removed from her presence whenever possible.

I suppose you could say my grandmother needed me. She was the only one who seemed pleased to have me near, and always saved chores, or favors as she called them, for me to do. Things like replacing the bulbs in her bedside lamps, or winding up the grandfather clock in the hallway. Many years passed before I realized that her servants could have done all of these things, and probably did when I wasn't around, but those 'favors' could have been the only thing that kept me from growing up a spoiled brat.

My grandmother made me feel needed, which in turn, made me feel loved. It was nice, feeling needed, and I suppose it felt nice knowing my skills as an actor were helping so many of my friends and coworkers here at RKM. Still, I wanted more. Surely Montgomery would be reasonable and let me do a couple of parts, as long as I promised to soldier on with Detective Tompkins? I suppose I didn't really hold out much hope for such a reversal of fortunes, but I refused to let negativity, otherwise known as reality, dampen my hopes.

When Douglas shouted "cut," I was able to stop my skulking through the green grass and the trees for a moment and take respite sitting on a park bench. I gratefully removed my hat and waved it in front of my face, adding to the breeze. I hoped my autopilot acting ability was good enough. Douglas seemed to be happy with my work, smiling as he spoke with the cameraman, so perhaps everything was all right there. This was a good sign. Whatever the outcome with Mr. Montgomery later in the day, everything was going to be just fine.

A voice cut through the silence. The tone was not, *hail thee fellow well met*, but rather, *oh, it's you, taking up space on my grassy lot.*

"Hello Theodore."

I looked up from my hat and found my greatest rival standing before me. Unfortunately Detective Tompkins was not the only cinematic sleuth that RKM Studios had to offer. To some, Lance Hudson was nearly as handsome as me, but with his pencil-thin mustache and slicked-back hair, he could've easily passed as a villain as well as a hero. Lance probably thought he was not only a hero, but that he should be the number one hero on the lot. Fortunately box office receipts continued to prove that my Detective Tompkins was more popular with the public than his *Case Files of Percy Wallace*. There were all sorts of theories why this was, but I had my own personal opinion. It stemmed from the actor himself. Despite our best efforts, our real personalities do come through in every character we play. In Lance's case, this included a bit of his pettiness and his genuine lack of good sportsmanship. For instance, Lance was sporting a sly smile, the type that did not bode well for anyone else, and I had a feeling the anyone else in question was me. If I had any sense at all I would immediately get up and run away, but the manners Mama had taught me ran deep. Despite my best intentions, I put my hat in my left hand, and stood up with my right hand outstretched to give Lance a proper greeting. "Hudson, I'm rather surprised to see you here."

"I had to come by for a visit, before you slipped off on your vacation next week."

I was sure he didn't spend his waking hours worried that I wasn't going to get my full rest during the seven days I had free between pictures. Something else was brewing beneath that calm actor's facade. "Oh?"

"Yes, I wanted to share with you this amusing photo I found today."

Hmm. Lance was looking quite like the canary that ate the cream. He had been searching for months to find a way to kick me off this a lot, and perhaps now he thought he had. "What photo?"

"Oh it's just a little snapshot, taken by a friend of mine last night near Mr. Montgomery's office."

Could one's heart actually jump right out of one's body? I imagined mine was on its way to the pavement right now. If Lance had a picture of me taken last night, it could only show one thing. "Oh really?"

"Yes. Take a look."

He handed it over and it confirmed my worst suspicions. It was a picture of me in my cleaning lady dress, my wig missing, with an expression on my face that made it look like I was running away from something. While it was a perfectly innocent photo, if someone looked at it without knowing the circumstances, they could imagine all sorts of disturbing scenarios. What reputation I had would be ruined in an instant, and here it was in the hands of my worst enemy. "I'm an actor on a movie set. It's not that strange for me to be seen in such an outfit."

"You know that, and I know that, Teddy," Lance said, sitting next to me, perching his ass on the edge of the seat, "but others might jump to some pretty nasty conclusions since you are wearing a dress. They might even wonder what type of person you are romantically inclined to spend time with after hours."

The threat was crystal clear. Gentlemen who spend time with gentlemen were frowned upon. Not that I spent any time with gentlemen, or with ladies really, in my off-hours. My love life was sort of nonexistent at the moment. Sally was my best friend. I trusted her implicitly, and I could share my deepest, darkest secrets with her, but she was more like the sister I wish I had. She was a far better person than the sister I was actually stuck with, but that was another story. As for sharing my bed, the only other living being in it at the moment was Penelope. If this photograph was passed around town, especially to the movie gossip queens, there was no question it would hurt my career. And as I had learned yesterday, if it hurt my career it would hurt other people at the studio as well. Lance of course cared nothing for his coworkers. He just couldn't stand not being top dog on the motion picture ladder. Well he wasn't going to get his wish.

Even though I wanted to branch out into other characters, I wasn't going to let Lance become the only detective on the lot. Not if I could do something about it, and I could. I had seen his type before. He was a bully, and there was only one way to be deal with a bully, and that was to be a bigger bully. I had thought he might come after me at some point in time, and I had contingency plans already in place. "You know Lance, my father came to visit last month, and while we were having lunch, your name came up."

The actor's eyebrows shot upward. Perhaps he was expecting me to scream, to shout, to send a fist toward his face. I had thrown him off guard, which was exactly what I wanted. "You did?"

"Oh yes. My father is on the acceptance committee for the Green Hills Country Club in Palm Beach. A country club where, if I recall correctly, your father is trying to become a member."

Lance leaned away from me, as his body grew rigid. Was I attacking him instead of being on the defensive? Lance spoke slowly and briefly. "Yes?"

I began to warm to my topic. "But your father is new money, isn't he? Money earned from the profits of his nation-wide chain of stores. I have grown up in country club societies my whole life, and I know how they frown upon new money."

"It's not fair." Whoa. Was that a hint of emotion from the normally stone-faced actor? Perhaps I had hit a nerve. "Just because he didn't inherit, doesn't mean his money isn't as good as anyone else's."

"I completely agree," I said. "I, after all, fled the country club life to come here to Hollywood. I'd much rather see a man earn his own way then live upon the backs of his ancestors. Still, I don't run the country club acceptance committee."

Finally, Lance began to understand. "But your father does?"

"Well," I said, trying to be humble. "I wouldn't say that he actually runs the committee, but his suggestions are taken seriously. If he proposes a candidate to become a member, they usually are accepted immediately, and if he opposes someone, they will never be allowed to join."

It was a risk I was taking. If Lance cared for his father as little as he cared for his coworkers, then that picture would be on the front pages within hours. I could only stop him if there was more than that little hint of emotion inside the man. I waited, only a century or two, while Lance said nothing. He just stared down at the photo, twisting it gently in his hands. Then, after the century expanded to a millennium, Lance tore the photo into two pieces. "I suppose we shouldn't let a picture like this go floating around, it might just give the wrong impression."

"That it might." I didn't give into victory just yet. "And other photos made from the same negative plates might give that impression as well. Do you know where the plates are?"

The actor pressed his lips tightly together, as if he was working hard to contain the words he wanted to let out so desperately. I was sure they were all very nasty words indeed. He spoke through grated teeth. "They are safe in my office. I will send them over to you by messenger just as soon as I get back."

"I appreciate that," I said, leaning back against the bench. I was glad I wore a dark suit today, as it hid the sweat trickling down my back. Victory often came with an emotional toll. "And I will speak with my father on the telephone later tonight. I will tell him what a fine fellow you are, and what a fine fellow your father must be as well. His nomination is all but assured, assuming," my voice hardened, "that the plates do actually arrive at my bungalow in a prompt fashion."

Oh, Lance was pissed, but he was backed into a corner and had no choice. "You have my word, you will get the plates."

I reached out to shake his hand. "Thank you, Lance. It is so nice knowing I have a friend like you on this lot."

If he swallowed the sour look on his face, he wouldn't be able to eat for year. Somehow I managed to keep from laughing as he stomped off my set. I wouldn't have to worry about a rival to Detective Tompkins. I was going to be the number one sleuth on this lot for quite some time to come.

***

A gust of wind blew against me, sending a chill around my chest. I tightened up my jacket. The sun that had been scorching me earlier was long gone, leaving a down-right biting cold in the air. The sidewalk was empty of all life. How late was it? A quick check of my pocket watch showed it was nearing eight o'clock. Hmm. Shooting had gone on a lot longer than I had realized.

When we finally wrapped for the day and for the film, I quickly changed my clothes and headed over to Montgomery's office determined not to leave until my demands were met. This was assuming he was still there, since I was visiting him after working hours again, but I couldn't scuttle and face Sally until I was sure I had missed him for the day. I wasn't really a coward, hoping I could put this off until sometime next week or really sometime next year, was I? *Drat it Teddy*, I told myself, *grow a backbone. You want this, you will go get it.*

Eight o'clock wasn't that late in the evening and there was still plenty of activity by the sound stages, but that was yards away. In the middle of the business side of RKM Studios, most of the office workers had gone home. I began to feel uneasy, traversing alone with the silent buildings watching over me, surrounded by dark trees, their branches oscillating in the gusty wind. It seemed like the buildings took on a personality of their own once the people were gone. The windows transformed into eyes, peering deep into the depths of the soul of any lone human foolish enough to wander into their midst. The swaying of the tree limbs was not caused by the breeze, but perhaps a more nefarious influence would command them to grab me and gobble me up before I could reach my destination—

Hmm. That might be a good scene in a horror movie. I would have to remember to tell Sally about it. She could make a grand script out of it I was sure. I was being silly anyway. RKM Studios was the safest spot in the otherwise topsy-turvy world. There was nothing to fear.

I reached the administration building and was about to climb the two short steps on the stoop when the front door flew open. A figure dressed in black from head to toe rushed out. Piercing blue eyes blazed in the darkness, while a scarf obscured the lower half of his face. An old scar cut through his left eyebrow. Something fluttered behind him—was he actually wearing a cape? Before I could get a really good look, he shoved past me and ran toward the trees. What the hell? My rump hit the pavement, hard.

"I say, there!" I shouted, but the fellow didn't stop. Didn't even look back. Seconds later he was gone. Why couldn't those darn trees reach out and grab him when I needed them to?

I struggled to my feet, brushing away the dirt and the grime. There'd better not be a rip in my new trousers. If they had to be fixed, who would pay the tailor's bill? Then I was struck with a far more important thought. Thank goodness I had left Penelope in my dressing room. She loved to ride atop my shoulders when we walked. Unlike other cats, I never had to worry about her losing her grip, or jumping away. She seemed to enjoy the view from atop of my six feet, and she enjoyed my company as well. But she would not have enjoyed a rough ride to the pavement. I would have been devastated if she had run away and I was unable to find her, all because of an idiot who couldn't watch where he was going.

Who was that bugger, anyway? His piercing blue eyes were vivid in my mind, but I knew no one who possessed such gems—I would have to find him and give him a proper dressing down.

More importantly, why in the world was someone running from the executive building in the dark of night, wearing a cape and a mask? Perhaps he was working on a thriller or one of those super hero-serials? No matter. Since I couldn't identify the bugger, the best thing to do if the trousers turned out to be damaged was to send them off to wardrobe for repairs.

I pushed through the front door. I had battled demon trees and a masked man to talk to my illustrious leader, and I was darn well going to do just that before calling it a day. Then I would return home to a warm fire, a brandy and Penelope snuggled up in my lap.

The outer office was empty, which at this late hour came as no surprise. I couldn't decide if I was pleased or disappointed to see the light spilling from the cracks around Montgomery's door. Despite my earlier determination, I was half hoping he had gone, but no such luck.

I scuffled closer and raised my hand to knock, and then I noticed the door was ajar. Strange, Montgomery always kept his office door securely shut. Everyone on the lot knew better than to walk right into the inner sanctum without being invited.

Even in my disguise as a cleaning lady, Montgomery's secretary had to knock politely and gain permission, before I could enter. It was no surprise that her desk was currently unmanned, given the lateness of the hour, but seeing that inner door open just a crack, that was unusual.

Now there probably was a very good explanation for why his door was ajar. Perhaps he was on his way out, was interrupted, then when he returned to the office to attend to one last detail, he left the door unlatched. But if that were the case, I would be hearing noise from within, wouldn't I? Some signs of life?

Dread overcame me. I had worked on enough whodunits to know what would happen next. I could picture the scene clearly. A giant movie mogul, pillar of the industry really, slumped over his desk. The large handle of a knife sticking prominently out of his back. Montgomery would have left a dying clue, perhaps part of a name, scrawled out on the desk top, written in his own blood?

Stop it! There went my imagination again, running around loose. I brushed my fingers against the wood, and lightly knocked on the doorjamb. The door shifted a bit, but I didn't want to push in uninvited. "Mr. Montgomery?" There was no answer.

You know the old wives tale was true. Those little hairs on the back of your neck do stand on end in disturbing situations. I told those little hairs there was nothing to fear. Of course Montgomery's body wouldn't be slumped over his desk. He was probably using the men's room down the hall and would be back any second, demanding an explanation for my apparent break-in. Then I remembered that Montgomery had his own water closet, right next to his private office. A perk for being an executive.

The dread returned. I called his name again, and got no

answer. Out of excuses to wait, I gave up and pushed the door open.

It wasn't exactly as I'd pictured it. There was no knife sticking out of Montgomery's back, no name scrawled in blood across the part of the desktop I could see, but I could only see part of the desktop. The rest of it was indeed covered by Montgomery's draping body, blood trickled down from a neat, round hole in the side of his forehead, and, oh yes, he was really dead.

So much for my overactive imagination.

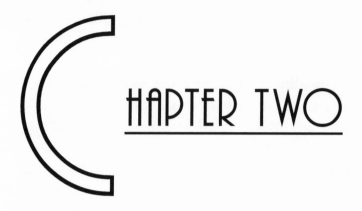

CHAPTER TWO

This was hardly the first dead body I had ever seen. That honor belonged to Smythson, my dear old friend. Guilt assailed me. I hadn't thought of him in years, yet his passing put a black mark on my soul which could never be fully erased. The mark flared back to life and suddenly I was no longer standing in the office of a very newly deceased movie mogul. I was back in the trenches of France, a very green and very terrified sixteen-year-old, surrounded by the booms of cannon fire crashing through the air. My nostrils were filled with the smell of gunpowder mixing with the sickening, coppery scent of blood and the retching odor of putrefying bodies. I gagged. It was all too vivid to be just a memory. It was real.

"Teddy."

I turned, and to my amazement, there was Smythson, standing complete and whole. He looked at me with that idiotic boyish smile that he never seemed to be without, even in the worst of times. A smile that only left his face when he was obliterated by a cannon.

"No!" I stared down at the horrifying mess that had been

my friend. The shock of it all had turned me stupid. Bullets and artillery flew all around me, lethal death just seconds away, but I just stood there. Unable to move or think of anything really at all.

"Wainwright, you idiot. Get down!"

I heard the command, but it seemed to be coming from so far away that it hardly registered. I didn't know how long I remained upright, but then arms wrapped tightly around me, pulling me to the ground. We had only just reached the safety of the dirt when a gigantic explosion blossomed violently just above us, showering us with clumps of mud and debris. My commander had saved me, but as I lay there and looked upon the unseeing eyes of Smythson, I knew nothing would ever be able to save my friend.

A human life had been lost, never to be retrieved. Irrevocably gone.

Smythson was the first, but he was soon followed by many others. It made me so damn mad that the lives of all those good young men, on both sides, wasted. Their futures ripped away for nothing. It was an anger I felt then, and it was that same fury I was feeling right now in Montgomery's office.

I don't know how long I stood there, gawking like an idiot. I suppose it was only a minute or two, but it seemed like forever. I shouldn't have been knocked for such a loop, but here I was.

Someone had taken Montgomery's life. Stolen years that could never be retrieved. Cut down a vital and energetic man in his prime. Whoever did this was going to have to pay, and I would do everything I could to make sure payment was swift and in full. I would mourn my employer later. Right now, I was going to concentrate on helping the police find his killer.

First off, I wasn't going to let all those years investigating fake crime scenes go to waste. I knew what to do, and more importantly, what not to do next. No rushing to touch the body. There was no reason to check for a pulse. A bullet wound to the temple was a fatal wound, period.

I hated films where the innocent person, upon discovering a dead body, would rush to pick up the conveniently placed gun, knife, or other murder weapon. Those scenes never rang true to me, because I never thought people could be so dumb. In this case, I wouldn't have been tempted, even if I were a blithering idiot. There was no conveniently placed gun lying around in plain view, and I wasn't about to snoop though Montgomery's office to see if I could find one. Right now the best thing I could do to help catch Montgomery's killer was to call for help.

I carefully backed out of the doorway, reached for the secretary's phone on her desk, and asked the operator to get me the police.

***

"You can make all the insinuations you like, Inspector Sheppard, but I did not kill R.K. Montgomery." I hadn't really been surprised when I was hauled down to the precinct house for the latest version of the third degree. The discoverer of the body always played a major role in these types of dramas. However, I was getting a little annoyed at the distinct lack of interest on the part of the police in the very real lead I had given them. Obviously my masked man was suspect number one. I did catch him fleeing the scene just minutes after the murder, yet the boys in blue seemed to be casting their focus elsewhere. Apparently on me.

After I had summoned the police to Montgomery's office,

I immediately placed another call to Sally. I had left Penelope alone in my dressing room and despite a cat's well-earned reputation for independence, I didn't want to leave her by herself for too long. Sally had promised to fetch Penelope immediately and then head home to await my call with further updates. I'd promised to phone again as soon as I could, and had hung up when the first wave of police arrived.

The first two who had showed up were the uniformed, patrol man type. They barked the usual orders at me, *don't move, don't breathe, did you kill him?* How I was supposed to answer their questions without breathing or moving was beyond me. I rooted my feet in the floor and proceeded to answer their questions promptly and fully, except for the one asking me to identify Montgomery's killer, which I couldn't answer since I didn't know.

Finally the adults arrived, and by adults I mean detectives. Three of them came into Montgomery's office, notebooks at the ready. The patrolmen jumped to attention, eager to impress the brass. With some careful eavesdropping I determined that the intrepid-looking man in front, probably in his early forties and wearing a two-dollar mail order suit and a fifty-cent cent hat, was one David Sheppard, inspector of the Los Angeles Police Department and the lead investigator.

He hadn't exactly seemed like a friendly fellow, but that was understandable. The man was investigating a murder, not attending a football rally. Still, Sheppard had seemed professional enough at first. He'd carefully examined the crime scene, asking the right questions of his men, but then something strange had happened. He caught sight of me.

I was used to seeing the glimmer in people's eyes when they recognized me on the street, and while my celebrity following wasn't nearly as intense with anyone over seventeen, or male, it still wasn't unreasonable to expect a similar reaction from some of the police. One assumed they go to the movies too. However, in those instances, usually one of two things happened. Either the person who had discovered I was actually in their presence rushed forward with outstretched arms asking for an autograph, or they were too shy to make an approach and just watched me carefully until I left their view.

Sheppard had done neither of these things. He'd recognized me alright, but there had been no sparkle of joy in his eyes. Instead he'd tensed up like a board, standing so stiffly I'd been afraid he might crack. That hadn't boded well. Still I wouldn't just remain silent when I had important information about the case, so I'd gone over there and introduced myself. The human board had just stood there, with his arms crossed, looking at everyone and everything in the room except me while I had tried to tell him about the masked intruder. When I'd finished, Sheppard said nothing. He had turned his back on me, leaving me for the underlings to handle.

I had done nothing to warrant this level of hostility, yet, after just one glance, apparently I had moved up into the exalted status of becoming suspect number one, at least in Sheppard's mind.

Now here I was, in a small room in the precinct house with a desperate need of an upgrade in decor, which was to say it needed some decor, of any kind. The only furniture in the room was one table and a couple of hard wooden chairs with no seat cushions. There was the obligatory strong, intense light placed on the stand directly opposite the table—a fixture in all interrogation scenes of course—and that was it. There was nothing as civilized as a rack to hang one's hat and coat, so I placed mine on a chair. I tried to act as naturally as possible. The other obligatory feature that the room had was a large mirror on the far wall. It wasn't just a mirror, it was a window. A window to my soul, or so the officers watching from the other side hoped.

Oh, goody.

I thought back to every crime movie I had ever seen, with the coppers pushing the bright lights into the bad guys' eyes, and beating him with a rubber hose. Even with myself now in the starring role of suspect, I wasn't unduly worried. I had seen my soul close up, and was quite familiar with nearly every aspect of it. Sure, I had an over active imagination. I liked to think up outlandish characters I wanted to play in the movies. I spent too much money on clothes and paid too much attention to my cat, but in one area there was no doubt. My killing days had ended at eleven o'clock on November 11th, 1918. There would be no more.

A couple of hours later I was no closer to convincing the inspector I was innocent.

While he ignored my attempts to talk to him earlier, now Sheppard was paying attention to me, and not in a good way. He asked me for the eighth time to recount the events of the evening, and I patiently obliged. I knew what he was doing. Ask the same questions over and over again, as he hoped to pounce on the tiniest of discrepancies. In my case, there were no discrepancies to find. The truth was my shield. I hadn't killed Montgomery. Inspector Sheppard could play whatever tricks he liked. There would not be a confession forthcoming, at least not from me.

This tactic of course, of only speaking the truth, did nothing to satisfy the inspector as he settled in to rendition number nine. "You admit you went to see the victim in disguise."

"Yes," I said, shifting in the hard chair a little. My bum was becoming a bit numb after all this time.

"Then you argued."

"We did not argue. We discussed my role at the studio."

Sheppard moved a fraction closer. He was such a mountain of intimidation. "What if I told you we had a witness who heard you argue?"

"Then, with all due respect, I would have to politely call you a liar." Really. Sheppard must have been getting desperate to make up such a story. "Even if Mr. Montgomery's secretary was there, and I do believe she had gone home by then, she could not have heard us arguing, because we did not argue."

Sheppard pulled back a little. "Montgomery rejected your proposal."

"Yes, and as I said, I was going back to try to change his mind. Despite your continued questioning, Inspector, you must know I didn't kill Montgomery." Regardless of the strange grudge he carried, I did not believe that Sheppard was a fool. "You won't find my prints on the murder weapon because it wasn't there. You found no gun on my person, and once your men dig a bit, you will discover that I do not own a weapon of any sort." I had had my fill of weapons sixteen years ago and intensely hoped the only gun I would ever touch again was of the prop variety. "You won't find my prints on R.K.'s person because I didn't touch him. You may find my prints on various items in his office because I picked them up when I was cleaning, as I have explained. As to motive yes Mr. Montgomery denied my request, but I was only asking to act in a minor role. I was disappointed, but not devastated and certainly not angry enough to kill the man." I grew more and more pleased with myself as I spoke. I had stated the case so well and listed my points so succinctly that perhaps I should join the bar, or star as a lawyer in my next picture. With the facts laid out so starkly, even the Inspector had to admit the evidence was flimsy at best, but perhaps he knew it already. "You don't really believe I killed R.K., do you? For some reason you don't like me, and you're letting your emotions cloud what I suspect are ordinarily exemplary judgment skills. Am I right?"

I was pushing my luck. Inspector Sheppard stood up, his fists clenched. Was he was seconds away from hitting me, or locking me up, lack of facts be damned? The inspector stood there for a second, his square jaw clenched as tight as his fist. After an eternity, he relaxed his jaw and his fists, turned on his heel, and left the room. Everyone else followed, leaving me alone with only the furniture for company.

Well, this could be a problem.

I had not yet been given the opportunity to contact a lawyer, or anyone for that matter. As the seconds turned to minutes, and the minutes turned into an hour, I wondered if I would ever get the opportunity. I passed the time picturing some future janitor, opening the door for the first time years from now, and finding my skeleton, still sitting in this very chair. At least my bottom wouldn't hurt anymore. The tender skin was on fire. I was about to risk getting up to stretch my legs, and blast anyone who was watching behind the mirror, when the door finally opened. In stepped a uniformed policeman telling me I was free to go.

I wasted no time putting on my coat and gathering my hat. Time to get out of there.

I made my way rapidly through the front lobby of the police precinct, eager to make my allowed-for escape. I spotted a star-struck look from a couple of the officers behind the front desk. Unlike the earlier policeman I had met, this pair must have really been fans of mine. Normally I would try to take time and say hello to anyone who spent some of their free time watching me cavort around on a movie screen, but it was two in the morning. I was tired, and eager to step out of the precinct and catch a breath of fresh, non-incarcerated air. I was just about to push my way through the barrier and out into freedom, when my highly attuned ear caught the rumble of voices on the other side. Lots and lots of voices. It seemed there was quite a tither going on out there. Oh dear, this could mean only one thing.

The press had arrived.

Someone must've leaked to the media that the police had taken me in for questioning. I wondered if it was one of Lance's spies, perhaps the same one who snapped that photo of me the other day. No matter who had given them the tip, I was going to be in a bit of trouble if I walked right into that lion's den.

Time for Plan B.

I turned around, plastered my best smile on my reportedly handsome face, and approached the two officers at the front desk. "Hello, I was wondering if you wouldn't mind if I borrowed a telephone for just a moment."

"Of course not, Mr. Wainwright!" One of the officers sent his chair crashing to the floor, he'd hopped out of it so fast. "It would be an honor." He gestured for me to come around to the other side of the desk, and then led me to the back of the room where there was a table lined with telephones. He seemed to be a bit nervous, as if he was afraid to ask me something.

I had seen that look many, many times before, and I had a feeling I knew what he wanted. "You are very nice to help me like this," I said. "Is there anything I can do to help you?"

His smile beamed like the sunlight. "My sixteen-year-old daughter, Clarabelle, is your biggest fan. She would think I was the greatest dad ever if I could bring home your autograph."

Clarabelle? I fought not to shutter. He would have to do

much, much more to appease her than just bring home my autograph. I do believe even a million dollars would not help compensate for saddling his daughter with such a name. Still, I was relieved that it would only cost me a scratch of my pen across a piece of paper to get some rescue. "Of course, I would be very happy to write a personal note to your daughter, right after I use the phone."

"Gee, that would be swell." Gee, I wondered who really was the sixteen-year-old in that family.

I lifted up the receiver, and listened to the lyrical tones of the operator girl on the other end. I gave her Sally's number, and while she connected us I wrote a note appropriate for six-teen-year-old fan.

Finally Sally's voice came over the phone line. "Teddy, are you alright? I've been so worried. What the hell have you gotten yourself into now?"

I winced, and briefly thought about hanging up the phone. Which was worse? Facing the hordes of press out the front, or Sally's wrath? Sanity stepped in at the last moment, help-ing me choose the right path. "I will explain everything later Sally, right now I need a ride."

"Are you still at the police precinct?"

"Yes, along with several of our friends from the newspapers and gossip sheets, all perched out front."

"Oh dear."

That was all Sally said, but I knew she immediately read the situation as well as I did. Being photographed leaving a police station in connection with the murder would almost be as bad as if Lance had published that picture of me in a dress. Upon second thought, maybe the picture of me in a dress would've been better after all. The press was here and they knew I was questioned by police in connection with the biggest murder to hit Tinseltown in years, but a photograph of me would make everything worse. "Hang on Sally." I turned to my new friend in blue, who was staring at the autograph I had written with awe. "I'm sorry I don't have a photo with me," I told him, pouring it on. "If you give me your address I'd be happy to send Clarabelle"—I internally shuddered again—"a photo inscribed directly to her."

"Gee, Mr. Wainwright, you are the greatest guy ever."

"Thank you." As he bent over to write the address, I asked for favor number two. "Say, is there a back way out of here?" I tried to seem casual. "I'd like to avoid those photo hounds out front if at all possible."

"Sure." He straightened up and handed me his address. "There's an alley out back. It's real easy to get to."

"Fantastic," I brought the phone receiver back to my ear. "Sally, I have a gentleman here who will give you directions so you can come pick me up."

I wouldn't have thought it possible, but his face seemed to blossom even more. "Gee," he said as he took the receiver from my hand. "No one has ever called me a gentleman before."

It was no wonder.

***

When I'd asked Sally to pick me up I should've realized if I didn't give her contrary instructions, like say, *head back to the lot to get my roadster out of the garage*, she would show up in her car.

A wicked wind blew past the front seat. I struggled to keep hold of my hat with one hand and pull Penelope close to me with the other. At least Sally had the good sense to wrap her in a rug. "I wish you would let me buy you a new automobile."

Sally tapped her fingers on the wheel, a true sign she was bored. This wasn't the first time we'd had this conversation. "First off, Teddy, I will buy my own cars with my own money, thank you very much. Second, there is nothing wrong with this one, it runs just fine."

"It's a Model T! While it may run just fine, it's missing a few things, like walls and heat."

She shook her head. Sally could be quite obstinate in some things. "Until the engine stops running, this will be my car."

"Yes ma'am," I gave up, for now, sat back, snuggled my cat, and tried not to freeze to death until we got to my apartment. All the excitement had caught up with me. My eyes were taking command, trying to close despite the cold and my best efforts to keep them open. I must've slept, because it took a squeal of the brakes and a jerk of the tires to rouse me. I blinked several times, and looked around.

"Hey," I protested. "This isn't my apartment building."

"Of course not," Sally said matter-of-factly. I didn't know how she did it, but she was always able to gracefully step out of her Model T, despite its height from the ground. Once she made it safely to the pavement, she grabbed a couple of newspapers from the backseat and headed toward the front stoop. "This is my apartment building, as you well know since you have been here before, although those visits were only in daylight hours. Your building has several visitors staked out both at the front and in the rear. I checked before I came over to pick you up."

I said a word I probably shouldn't have, but Sally was the daughter of a US Army sergeant, and I was sure she had heard worse. Apparently I was the juicy story of the moment, and I really didn't like it. I carefully bundled Penelope into my arms, then climbed onto the wide running board before hopping to the ground. I followed Sally toward the front door, and I stopped short when something else I didn't like occurred to me. "You don't expect me to go in there with you, do you?"

She opened the lobby door. "Of course I do. Where else are you going to go at three in the morning?"

"I, and by that I mean, I alone, could go to a hotel, a motor inn, anything. Sally, you're a single woman, I can't sleep in your apartment without a chaperone present. It isn't proper."

Sally let the door close, and gently patted my cheek. "My dear Teddy, you are such an innocent. Of course you'll be sleeping on the couch. You know full well what would happen if you tried to get any closer to my bedroom than that."

I shuddered, recalling a crisp summer day on an Oahu beach where, under her father's tutelage, Sally broke a stack of wooden planks with her bare hand. Karate, I think they called it, or was it judo? I couldn't be sure. I was sure that when it came to self-defence, Sally was the better equipped of us both, and could handle any situation. "Now Sally, you know I would never try such a thing." I valued my bones, especially those in my arms and legs, whole and intact. "It's your reputation I'm worried about."

"I'm more worried about your reputation in connection with R.K.'s murder. Getting you off the streets and out of the eye of the press is the most important thing right now and before you bring up the hotel or motel idea again, consider this. Those places have people on the front desk. People who would recognize you. People who have access to telephones and are willing to earn a little extra cash by giving a local reporter a scoop. We can't risk it."

"Well I suppose," I gave in on this like everything else when it came to Sally and her common sense. It looked like Penelope and I were to be her house guests. "But only for one night,"

I said, reasserting my manliness. "Tomorrow we're going to have to figure out something else."

"Yes, Theodore."

Dammit, how could a woman be so supportive and so condescending at the same time? It was a never-ending mystery, but somehow Sally seemed to manage it often. She returned to the lobby door, then stopped and turned toward me once again, sprouting a smile that could only be described as wicked. "Besides, I quite like the idea of the neighbors thinking I have brought a man home for the evening. It's just the kind of gossip those old harpies need."

"Sally." How could I not laugh at such logic? I followed her up the steps. "You are a one-of-a-kind."

"Thank goodness for that," she replied.

Thank goodness indeed.

***

Sally lived in a small, one bedroom apartment on Willoughby Avenue nestled between Santa Monica Boulevard and Melrose. It was a far cry from the palace she grew up in, but she said she liked it better because she paid for it herself. The apartment was a split level unit, boasting a combined living room and kitchen, and it also had a bedroom up the one flight of stairs. It was located on the edge of the Hollywood district. Any further south and it would take her too long to get to the studio, either by automobile or by electric trolley.

I deposited Penelope onto the couch. She and I were apparently were to share our sleeping accommodations, and I settled down beside her. It had been a long night after an even longer day. So much had happened since Lance's clumsy attempt at blackmail, it was almost as if weeks had passed, instead of a few hours. It was a good thing those photographic plates had been delivered to my bungalow as promised. Even if Lance wanted to help his father, I doubt he would have been able to resist adding to my troubles now that I was mixed up in a murder.

Sitting on the couch had been a mistake. The adrenaline I had generated because of the events of the day was ebbing away, leaving me exhausted, and apparently hungry. My stomach rumbled just then, with a volume loud enough to match one of Penelope's purrs. "Hey Sally. Got anything to eat?"

"Of course." She carefully hung up her coat in the closet and headed toward the tiny kitchen. "I have some leftover spaghetti I can heat up in a jiff if you'd like."

My mouth watered. Did I mention Sally cooked as well as she did everything else? "That sounds perfect, if you're not too tired."

"No indeed. I had a nice nap earlier this evening, before I heard the news about poor Mr. Montgomery. I am quite refreshed now."

"In that case, thank you."

"My pleasure."

I leaned back and was about to close my eyes when a newspaper smacked me in the face. Startled, I flailed my arms in an attempt to catch the sliding newsprint. In the process, I jostled Penelope, who jumped off the couch, hissing her displeasure. "Sorry, my love," I tried to appease her with a pet, but she was having none of it. She scuttled under the desk chair and glared at me with eyes suddenly possessed with malevolence. I sent a matching glare toward Sally, who was laughing at us both. "What was this all about?" I waved the newspaper, clutched in my hand with a death grip, toward her.

"If you fall asleep before I'm done with the spaghetti I'll never get you awake enough to eat."

"So you keep me alert by assaulting me with a newspaper?"

"That's not just any paper. I stopped by the newsstand to pick up a couple of the early editions on my way over to the police station. You'd better take a look at the front pages."

I sank back onto the couch. As Sally returned to the kitchen to complete preparations for my meal, I released my grip on the newsprint. Surely the headlines wouldn't be too hysterical?

Surely the could.

Each headline screamed the story in large print across the front page. One said: "*Movie Mogul Murdered: Film Star Theodore Wainwright Finds Body.*" I forced myself to remain calm, and read the entire article. While they didn't come right out and say I murdered Montgomery, there was plenty of innuendo if one was willing to read between the lines. I groaned.

"Cheer up," Sally called out from the stove. "I'm sure the story has gone nationwide by now. You mother is sure to read it tomorrow morning when she breaks her fast with clotted cream and jam."

I groaned again. This was just getting better and better. I flung the paper aside, and glanced at Penelope. She was still staring daggers at me, so I was to get no moral support from that quarter. I tried to decide who had it worse, Montgomery or me. Of course, that wasn't really a fair analogy—the man was dead after all, but at least he didn't have to worry about anything anymore. The adrenaline returned with a rush, pushing my fatigue away. I needed to figure out what to do next.

I didn't have to try very hard. I had been subconsciously plotting a course of action ever since I'd seen Montgomery slumped over that desk. All I needed to do now was to work out the details, a task I had accomplished by the time Sally called me to the table. She placed a heaping plate full of spaghetti in front of me, and sat across the table cradling a cup full of tea, content to keep me company while I ate.

"We need to go back to the studio tomorrow," I told her between bites.

"Back to the studio? Whatever for? You don't start your next picture for another week."

"I need to work on a different job."

"What kind of job?"

"Well, since the press has already decided that I am guilty of Montgomery's murder, there really is only one thing to do. Find the real killer before I get sent to the electric chair on trumped-up charges."

Sally's fingers lost a bit of their grip around her cup, and she nearly spilled her tea. "You're going to find the real killer? How?"

I thought of the person I had run into in front of Montgomery's office. The caped crusader—or potentially, the masked murdered. "I have an idea where to start."

CHAPTER THREE

A pair of arms suddenly wrapped around me, preventing me from moving forward. I flailed and wiggled, fighting to get free, yet I only managed to send a cloud of sequins flying into the air. Finally, with a grunt of disgust, I worked myself loose of the bejeweled evening gown, worn in the 1932 musical "*Tapping with my Feet*," a classic. There was no one in the dress; I had been assaulted by the garment alone.

First a girdle, and now this. My luck with women's wear was getting worse and worse.

I wanted to fling the wretched obstacle away, but I couldn't treat a piece of Hollywood history in such a disrespectful manner. Instead, I gently straightened the shoulders around the hanger and returned it to its proper place on a wardrobe rack.

When I'd woken up on Sally's couch that morning I was pleased to find that sometime during the night, Penelope had nestled on top of my chest. She had forgiven me, and that was the last bit of good news I had for a while. I placed a call to the caretaker of my ranch in the San Fernando Valley. That was where I had been planning on spending my week off, but

Fernandez told me the bad news. A couple of guys wearing hats, with the word *press* tucked into their bands, were skulking about. Apparently representatives of the fourth estate decided to risk driving the hazardous roads from Hollywood to the San Fernando Valley in the hopes of tracking me down and getting a prime scoop. I was becoming one of the most wanted men in the city, a situation which didn't appeal to me in the least. I had to do something immediately, and apparently that something meant dancing with a dress.

I made sure that the gown was hanging correctly, with nary a wrinkle, and then continued my journey deep into the bowels of RKM Studios' costume department. "What was that number again?"

"Section nine," Sally shouted from somewhere behind me. "Aisle twenty-five, item number four hundred thirteen."

"It would have thirteen in the number," I muttered. "It's so unlucky." I pushed garment after garment out of my way as I struggled to make progress through the hundreds of clothing racks that filled the room. At first, it seemed I was taking on an impossible task. Every costume ever worn on every RKM film was stored in this warehouse. It added up to more than thirty thousand costumes in the studio's fifteen year history. So there we were, surrounded by acres and acres of beaded dresses, black tights, and feather headdresses. How in the devil was I going to find one particular costume in this giant clothing extravaganza?

When Sally and I had arrived at the studio that morning, we had given Montgomery's office a wide berth. I had chatted with Bernie, the guy who guarded the main gate, and he told me there were plenty of men in blue still sniffing around that area. I had wondered, and secretly hoped, there would also be a contingent of police at the wardrobe department, but unfortunately it seemed to be only business as usual there. Oh, there were a few costume designers and actors coming and going, but no sign of an official presence. Drat it all. Sheppard must have ignored the clue I had given him, but I wasn't going to. Sure, a movie lot was full of people walking around, wearing kooky and crazy costumes at all hours of the day or night. Even so, I found it hard to believe that a man in a mask and cape, literally crashing into me on the steps leading to a crime scene, was a coincidence or an innocent act. Since most people didn't have a mask and a cape lying around the house, most likely he was wearing a costume. A costume that probably came from here.

"I've found garment three-fifty," I shouted to Sally, working my way forward. She had been looking in the aisle next to mine, but now I heard the rustle of fabric as she changed course moved toward me. "four-eleven, four-twelve," I was getting close. Then I found a very obvious gap between the hangers. "Sally?"

"I'm here." Slightly out of breath, she caught up with me. She nodded toward the gap. "You were right. Your suspect did take the costume from '*The Legend of the Masked Avenger*' film."

I nodded. "A dreadful serial, full of tripe. A bizarre story line about characters as exciting as wet cardboard, each of whom was running around wearing the most ridiculous of outfits. Embarrassing, really."

"This from someone who wants to be known as 'The Man of a Thousand Disguises'?"

Oh, how Sally enjoyed poking fun at what she considered to be my weaknesses.

"All right," I conceded, "point taken." My finger marked the gap on the rack. My first real clue. "Thank goodness for Wardrobe Mistress Esther's extensive index card reference system. Without it, we would have never have been able to prove that a costume had been taken without properly being recorded on file."

"Even if you assume that the person you bumped into was really R.K.'s killer, how does this"—she pointed to the gap—"help us catch him?"

"Don't you see? Whoever took this costume has to be familiar with the wardrobe department."

"Which means he has to be familiar with the inner workings of a movie lot."

"Exactly." I thought back to the encounter: the caped man's piercing blue eyes, his scar, and the way he carried himself. "That fellow wasn't just wearing a costume. He was living the role of the Masked Avenger. Our culprit must be an actor."

"I don't want to dampen your excitement Teddy," said Sally as she proceeded to do just that, "but there are hundreds, if not thousands of actors on this lot, all of whom are familiar with the workings of this wardrobe department." She touched my arm. It was her nonverbal way of saying she thought I was being a blithering idiot again, yet she was still supporting me and my wild ideas. "How can you find him? You didn't see his face."

"No," I replied, "but I'll never forget those piercing blue eyes, and his scar. If I can get close enough, I'll recognize him."

"And how do you expect to get close enough? You're the star of the lot Teddy. You might gain a bad reputation if you go around grabbing the head of everyone you pass and pulling their face toward yours to get a good look."

"Sally." She could be so silly at times, but she did have a point. How could I possibly get close enough to our killer to identify him, without getting arrested for some improper behavior myself?

I eyed the thousands of costumes and a wild and ridiculous idea came to me. Could it really be so easy? Could I fulfill two of my desires at the same time?

Perhaps I could.

***

Blast it. I hadn't realized it was going to be such a struggle, trying to get around with only one eye to see with. Where the hell had that tree come from? I had made the mistake of looking down at my cobbled-together shoes for just an instant and when I looked back up, there it was. The mighty oak seemed to have moved from the park all by itself, and had magically appeared right in the middle of the sidewalk. I was seconds away from smacking right into it, when with some flailing of the arms and some straightening of the spine, I was able to stop just in time. I looked around and saw with my one good eye that the tree had not moved, I had wandered off course. A near disaster, all because I could only partially see! I wondered why pirates had to wear these patches anyway. Blocked vision certainly wouldn't aid them in their plundering, and it wasn't doing much to aid me in my detecting either. I straightened, shoved hands casually into my pocket, and whistled a jaunty jig as I walked. The loud *click-clack* of my shoes became a grand compliment to the music coming from my mouth, or so I chose to believe. *Avast ye maties*, I thought. *Pirates be here.*

After Sally and I had finished in the wardrobe department, I'd realized if I was going to properly implement my new plan, I was going to need help, and to get that help, I was going to need a bribe. Sally had to get back to work, so we'd parted ways and I'd headed for my bungalow. When I'd gotten inside, I'd greeted my cat properly, and then headed for the closet. As soon as I'd opened the closet door, Penelope was inside, inspecting every item stuffed within. I had to work around her squirming body to do my own search, but finally I was able to find the very expensive and very rare bottle of scotch I had stashed away for emergencies.

This was an emergency.

Penelope had finished her inspection and decided to curl up on top of a quilt, made by Sally's mother, and take a nap. Seeing she would be comfortable for the foreseeable future, I'd left her snoozing, and headed back to the wardrobe department. Once there I'd located Esther, our wardrobe mistress, and waited patiently while she enjoyed a taste or two of the scotch. Alright, maybe it was more than two. After most of her glass had been emptied, she turned into a very pleasant wardrobe mistress indeed, and consented to give me free reign of the cavernous department. I now had permission to borrow any costume I wished, without a record kept, and I was going to need a lot of costumes.

Sally was quite right when she said I was going to have to get close to people if I was to have any hope in identifying our killer. She was also quite right believing I couldn't conduct this search as myself. Even if I didn't take into account the press and the police, who were constantly on my trail, being noticed wherever I went was not a situation that would lend itself to successful undercover work. No, if I was to have any chance at all in uncovering our killer, Theodore Wainwright was going to have to disappear. I would have to become someone else. I would have to become the Man of a Thousand Disguises—or at least, the Man of Six or Seven Disguises.

There were seven movies currently shooting at RKM, and I might have to infiltrate them all before I was through. Sally knew everything about the comings and goings around the lot, so she gave me a quick rundown of the films that were currently in production. They ranged from westerns, to a rather adult romance, to a science fiction serial for the young ones. Each of those venerable productions came complete with a cast and crew that could number up into the hundreds.

Where to start? One was just as likely as another as far as finding my Masked Avenger was concerned, so I picked the film that looked like the most fun. Pirate movies were popular at the moment, thanks to a cinematic star who shall not be named, since he worked at another studio. Since RKM was not to be outdone by anyone, we were filming our own little version of a swashbuckler. While I was probably the only human on the planet not impressed by that other pirate fellow across town, I did love swashbucklers. Maybe it was because my mother didn't approve of such material, and therefore I always enjoyed sneaking to the attic to read about Blackbeard and buried treasure. Ah, those were the days.

So now, dressed in proper buccaneer's ensemble, I was headed for the set, just one of the many extras on his way to work. My one eye kept a stern lookout for further obstacles to be avoided, and for any suspicious glances directed at me. While my outfit wasn't authentic to the period, my striped shirt with matching knee socks, brown pants that ended just below the knee, scarf carefully wrapped around my head, phony cheeks attached to my face to make it rounder and finally that aforementioned blasted patch, all served to disguise my features quite admirably. But would it be enough? I had to fool people I knew, and some I worked with every day. Would I be recognized?

I faced my first challenge almost at once. I was heading toward Studio 8B, where today's filming was scheduled, when I nearly ran into a gentleman holding a cup of coffee. "Hey, watch it, you," he said with the air of a man who expected his orders to be followed immediately.

Oh, drat it. This was indeed a man used to command. I had literally run into Inspector Sheppard, and had almost spilled hot coffee down the front of his trousers. I immediately felt like a criminal, ready to take to my heels to escape the long arm of the law. Fortunately sanity reasserted itself before I ruined my whole life. I had done nothing wrong, but running would make it look like I did.

Sheppard clutched the coffee cup with one hand, while the other pulled a handkerchief out of his breast pocket. He dabbed the damp spots, created by the overflowing liquid. He barely glanced at me while he did this. To him, I was not a threat. Nor, perhaps, an acquaintance. I didn't think he recognized me.

Time to steel up the nerves, like I had done during the war. I knew it would be a challenge to act naturally the first time I bumped into someone I knew while in disguise, but I didn't think my acting skills would be put to the test against a man who could lock me up for years on end. A man trained to sniff out deception and guile. Still, this was the situation and it was time to face it head on.

"Sorry mate," I muttered in a gravely voice, tinged with a British accent for good measure.

Sheppard wrinkled his nose. There was a hint of alcohol on my breath, but fortunately Prohibition had been repealed a few years back, so he couldn't run me in for drinking. I thought it added flare to my character.

I dared to give Sheppard my best leer. The inspector reared back a step or two, and more liquid spilled from his cup. Sheppard grimaced, and then threw his cup into a nearby garbage can.

"You need to be more careful," he ordered.

"Aye aye, sir," I flashed him my snappiest salute. "Anything you say."

Sheppard kept his eyes on me for a moment as he slowly backed away, and then headed toward the parking lot. I wondered if he was enjoying his behind-the-scenes look at a working motion-picture lot, but it didn't matter. He didn't recognize me at all. I had passed my first test.

Encouraged by my success, I raced toward the mighty Pacific Ocean, which in reality was only a couple of hundred feet wide. A few years back Montgomery had built a lagoon on the back lot. It served as a double for every waterway required by a script, be it a pond, river, or sea. On this day I found a pirate shipwreck built on the phony sands at the edge of the lagoon, with the camera, lights, and sound equipment clustered just in front of it.

I slipped in and joined a crowd of extras milling around. Nobody paid me any attention. Some people were looking at copies of the script, while others were adjusting their costumes and makeup, and I caught sight of a couple of guys in the back having a little snort. It warmed my heart to see that Wardrobe Mistress Esther wasn't the only one partial to good alcohol.

Although I tried not to be too obvious, I closely studied the face of every person I came across as I made my way through the crowd. Some people had blue eyes of course, but none were quite the shade of piercing blue I was looking for. Nor was there any sign of a scar on anyone's eyebrows. I thought I had checked nearly everyone in the area when the director began to shout, stirring people into action. It seemed they were beginning some sort of fight scene.

"Hey you!" A young man, who had hair flying at all angles,

and glasses barely hanging on to his nose, ran up to me. He held a clipboard. "Where's your cutlass?"

While I had envisioned my disguise with meticulous detail, I hadn't actually included any weaponry. A mistake, apparently. "Sorry," I said. "I guess I lost it."

"Stupid extras," the man muttered, and added a few other choice words, best not to be repeated. He ran to a nearby prop crate, flipped the top open and grabbed the first wooden sword sitting on top of a pile inside, and shoved the weapon toward me.

"But this is a copy of a nineteenth-century dueling sword," I protested as he pushed me toward the crowd. "It's not historically accurate for this time period."

"I don't care. The director is going to call action any minute." He pushed me hard, sending me stumbling toward the rest of the extras. "Now get ready to fight!"

"Yes sir."

As the man with the clipboard hurried away, I was surrounded by a group of blood-thirsty cutthroats about to do battle. I hadn't read the script and had no idea how the scene was supposed to go, but who cared?

The director called action, and I surged ahead with the rest of the fellas, crying out, flailing, and swinging my sword with the best of them. Real battlefields were no place to be, but fighting in a fake one? There was no better fun in the world.

***

I emerged from the battle victorious, but still no closer to finding my man in the cape. A whole day had gone by and it was time to make arrangements for the night. I left the comfort of Sally's couch and checked into a pet-friendly hotel nestled in a secluded section of Beverly Hills. It was a hotel known for its discretion, since most of its clientele were either very wealthy or very famous. Sally didn't need to worry about bell-hops or desk clerks tipping off the press to my presence. No reporter could match the salary the staff was making there. I would be safe. They also loved Penelope and treated her like the queen she was, an extra plus.

Sally, of course, wanted me to continue staying at her place but I wouldn't have it. One night in emergency circumstances was barely acceptable, any more than that was just asking for trouble. So I indulged myself by lying on top of the bed in my casual attire. This meant trading in my suit coat for a dressing gown, exchanging my street shoes for slippers, and loosening my tie. Over my lap was a bed tray, containing the finest steak, baked potato, vegetables, and coffee that room service had to offer. They even provided a can of tuna for Penelope, along with a saucer of milk. After dinner, I relaxed by reading a book, then it was off to la-la land for eight hours of decidedly blissful sleep. When morning came, it was back to the studio for more detecting.

Next up, I infiltrated one of those steamy divorcee pictures. I decided that I desperately needed to be a Latin lover for a day, so after some whispered consultation with Wardrobe Mistress Esther, I emerged from her dressing room wearing gaucho pants, a matching gaucho hat, a white shirt, a black vest, and adorning my face was a pencil-thin mustache along with a goatee. I thought about clenching a rose between my teeth, but didn't want to attract too much attention. It would be difficult to conduct an undercover investigation with every woman on the set swooning over me. I managed to infiltrate the film successfully and spent the day dancing in a ficti-tious nightclub. While I got no closer to my quarry, I did learn a few new steps.

I also got an education in other, more titillating matters. I was shocked by the somewhat scandalous nature of the women in the film. While I was not a prude by any means, watching the main character, a divorcee, actually proposition a young man and invite him home to see her etchings was quite a spark to the imagination. Along with a spark to ticket sales, I assumed.

As a rule sex sells, but perhaps for not much longer. A few years ago, a decency code had been inflicted upon studios in Hollywood. Certain conservative types in Washington had been expressing their displeasure about the so-called "loose" morals on display in motion pictures. When they threatened to pass new laws imposing strict decency rules, Hollywood beat them to the punch. Some studios followed the new code, cleaning up their own house in an effort to keep the government from doing it for them.

In the scene currently being filmed, the divorcee had gotten her young man on the couch. Obviously such decency rules didn't apply here. At RKM Studios any signs of decency were long gone.

It was late when filming wrapped on the divorcee set. Still in my Latin garb, I ventured toward the writers' bungalow. No point in wasting a Latin lover outfit without giving Sally a chance to laugh at me before I changed.

She didn't laugh, however, when I arrived. She hardly glanced at me, she was so busy typing. Sally was surrounded by a mountain of white. All scripts I presumed. I had never seen so much paper stacked on her desk before. "Sally, what's going on?"

"Oh Teddy," she said without looking up. "I've suddenly been assigned to rewrite at least ten scripts, and all are under deadline."

"I don't understand? I thought you were nearly caught up with all your work?"

"That was before Mr. Farnsworth arrived, with his mighty stack of changes and—what are you wearing?"

I struck an appropriate pose and grasped her hand, snatching her from behind the desk. Together we tangoed across the room. "I am the world's greatest Latin lover. One dance with me, and you will be under my spell forever."

"Teddy," she giggled. "You are a gigantic flirt."

"I know," I said, happy I at least got her to laugh, just a little.

Her smile began to fade. "I'm sorry, but I don't have time for this." She pulled away and returned to her desk.

I followed her. "You mentioned something about Farnsworth, the censor." I thought back to Montgomery's dictation when I was dusting his office. I didn't know much about the fellow, but I'd heard he'd been an actor back in the day. There must have been more money in telling people what to do, rather than doing it himself. "I thought censors were banned from the lot?" There was certainly no sign of censorship on the divorcee set.

"That was before Mr. Montgomery died," Sally sighed. "Mr. Owens is now running the studio for the time being, and it seems he does not possess the backbone that Mr. Montgomery had. Mr. Owens has given Mr. Farnsworth complete access to the studio, and has turned my life upside down."

"I'm so sorry," I kissed her cheek. "Shall I come by later with some food for you?"

"I look forward to it."

I was just about to leave when the door crashed open, and I blinked to make sure I wasn't seeing things. Harvey Spencer stumbled through the doorway. It had been so long since the head writer had actually been in the office. No, Spencer was really there, staggering toward his desk. The situation must have been dire if he was roused from his drunken slumber to do some work.

"Hurry up Sally," he tried to say, his words slurring only a little. "You have to get those pages turned in within the hour."

"Yes, Mr. Spencer," Sally replied. "I'll see you later, Teddy."

I didn't care for the situation, but I couldn't see a way for my presence to make anything better at the moment. I waved goodbye and returned to my bungalow. I took a moment to make sure nobody noticed me slipping inside, as I didn't want anyone to take any more suspicious photos.

As I removed my gaucho pants, I pondered the changes facing the lot without Montgomery at the helm. It seemed like the apparent debauchery on the divorcee set was the last film of that kind we would be making for a long time. While it was too early to say if that was a good or a bad thing, now with someone watching over every word we said, combined with a murderer still on the loose, it didn't bode well for the future. Not well at all.

***

Despite my worries, I slept soundly, and after more room service—it wouldn't do to go to the dining room for breakfast since I was trying to keep a low profile—I dressed in everything except my suit coat and sat in the easy chair by my hotel room window to catch the light while I read the morning headlines. I wanted to catch up on the latest details surrounding the scintillating R.K. Montgomery murder case, but unfortunately there were no new details to catch up on. Discounting the continuing speculation that yours truly was involved—the fourth estate was getting peeved that they couldn't find me, which suited me just fine—there seemed to be little progress in the case.

Apparently the juiciest item the paper had to offer was that

Sheppard's boys still had Montgomery's office sealed off. Not so juicy an item, really. The police should have vacuumed all the clues out of that room by now. The fact that they were still there meant they had no place better to be. I scanned the back pages, hoping to find some sort of news, but nothing. There was no word on if a weapon was found, no word about anyone making recent threats against the movie mogul, no word if any other suspect had moved from secondary to prime position. Basically, there was no word. It looked like it was back to the makeup table for me.

Today I would visit the Wild West. As my search continued, my choice of films to infiltrate was narrowing. It was only a matter of time before I had to breech the set of *The Case Files of Percy Wallace* and facing Lance would be the ultimate challenge. He'd already seen me in a dress. Would he be able to penetrate any other disguise I could come up with?

There was no point in thinking about that now. I had a killer to catch. And it was time to play cowboy.

***

Two hours later I sauntered onto the western set dressed to the hilt as an ole cowpoke. My face sported a nose twice as wide as my own, and eyebrows twice as bushy. My hair was now long, stringy, and a dirty, washy brown—fortunately most of it was hidden beneath a ten-gallon hat. My cowboy boots pinched my toes, and had spurs that threatened to dig into the ground with every step. As I walked, or tried to walk without my spurs tangling, I gave the horses on set a wide berth. I loved animals, including horses, but for some reason the horses didn't love me. They tried to bite me whenever I got within range. I didn't know why, but it always happened.

As I stood there listening to one whinny, I resigned myself to the fact that a horse and I would never be friends, and moved on with my life, or at least to the craft table for a donut.

As I mingled with the extras, I caught the glance of a fellow rapidly heading my way. Apparently I was standing between him and the restroom. This by itself was not extraordinary. Often people were trapped on the set for long hours, without a break, and on occasion I had to hold it in for quite some time. There was often a rush for the toilets when the camera stopped rolling. Apparently this fellow had waited almost too long. I tried to move out of the way, but I didn't shift fast enough and he crashed into my left side. Knocked off balance, I nearly toppled over and instinctively I latched onto his vest in an effort to remain upright. When I had regained control, I looked up, and stared right into the piercing blue eyes I had been searching for. There was even a scar over his left brow.

I had found him.

He was also dressed in western wear, though if he was an extra or a principle actor on the film I couldn't tell. I certainly didn't recognize him, and I knew most of the major players on our lot, but there was no question in my mind. This is the person I'd seen fleeing Montgomery's office dressed as the Masked Avenger. A smile curved my lips, but I tamped it back down. He wasn't supposed to know how happy I was to see him.

Although, I wasn't so happy anyway. Sure, I had found him, now what was I supposed to do with him?

He decided for me. "Watch it," he spat. "You're standing in my way."

Hmm. Not only was my man a possible murderer, he was grumpy as hell. "Sorry."

He didn't seem impressed with my attempt at atonement, yet he didn't seem alarmed at my presence either. I didn't seem to matter to him at all, except as an annoyance. With a last, disgruntled glance, he hurried away, but he didn't leave alone.

He was ridiculously easy to follow. After a proper interval in the men's room to let nature take its course, he reappeared and headed straight for the commissary, this time at a much more leisurely pace. Once he had gotten his coffee, he sat comfortably right across from a wall mirror. He gave his reflection the kind of adoring looks one gives a lover. Interesting.

I dithered for moment, torn. Part of me wanted to run right over to Montgomery's office, where the police were still hanging about, and get some help, but I was terribly afraid the man would be gone by the time we returned. I had to try to get some information about him, any information, before letting him out of my sight.

Determined, I got my own coffee, and then approached his table. He was still paying more attention to the mirror than to his drink, which seemed so strange that I decided to try something. I sat down across from him, blocking his view. "Listen fella, I'm sorry I bumped into you before. Let me make it up to you."

He kept shifting from side to side, trying to get a better view of the mirror. "That's okay," he said quickly, tapping his fingers on his cup. "I'm fine. You can move along now."

He was about to shift to a different seat, leaving me with nothing. Drat it. I had to stall him. "Say, I've seen you around the lot before. You must be starring in that cowboy picture."

He stopped his squirming and stared at me. "You think I'm the star?"

"Yes," I promised to forgive myself later for lying. "I saw you strutting—I mean walking—around the set, and since you are obviously the most handsome man there, I just assumed you were staring in the picture."

"I should be," he fumed, "but that casting director must be blind. Right now I'm only an extra."

"That's terrible," I said, sending a mental apology to Timothy. "I am sure your face will be prominently displayed on the covers of the Hollywood gossip magazines soon." I saw an opening to get some information, so I jumped in and grabbed it. "What is your name? I want to be able to tell my friends I met you when you show up in all the papers."

He smiled, now happy for my interest. "It's Harrington. Chad Harrington."

"Glad to know you," I said, offering a hand.

He hesitated for just a second before shaking my hand eagerly. "I have to rush back to the set now and start working on the director. The more he gets to know me, the shorter the time will be before he gives me a bigger part." Harrington stood up and looked down at me. "Remember this day. It's the day you met Chad Harrington." He smiled again, and walked off.

As soon as he was out the door, I hastily leapt to my feet and raced toward the administration building. I wanted to talk about Harrington to one special friend right now, and his name was Inspector Sheppard.

I was halfway to the offices when I remembered I was still dressed as a cowboy. While Inspector Sheppard wasn't my greatest fan, he would be more likely to listen to me than a random cowboy, wouldn't he?

Every second I dithered gave Harrington more time to get away. Not that I really thought he would try to run. He was probably doing exactly what he said he would, heading right back to that set, but I couldn't risk it. I had to talk to Sheppard right now.

I ran to the nearest garbage can. There I removed my stringy brown hair, and ripped the putty off my nose and the bushy eyebrows off my face, and threw them in the trash. Then I placed the ten-gallon hat on a nearby bench. Hopefully no one would take it while I was gone. Wardrobe Mistress Esther would be upset with me if I lost it, but I had to risk it. I couldn't do much about the rest of my clothes, but at least my head and my face was now my own.

Rushing toward the administration building, I was relieved to see the inspector standing in front, flipping through a notebook. "Inspector Sheppard," I called out. "Wait!"

Police officers must have had good hearing, because even though he was rather far away, he heard me. He looked up, and his jaw dropped. I imagine I was quite a sight, a cowboy running full tilt toward him, spurs jangling every time they hit the pavement. Sheppard didn't move. He didn't pull his gun, didn't walk away. He simply waited.

I reached his side, gasping for breath, fighting to speak. "Inspector Sheppard, I found him."

"Found who?" To his credit he didn't seem to react to the sight of me in such outlandish clothes. "You found the killer?"

"Yes, he's on the cowboy set right now." I grabbed his arm and started tugging him across the parking lot. "If we hurry, we can catch him."

The inspector wasn't exactly resisting my advances, but he wasn't running eagerly by my side either. "Wait a minute. How do you know he's the killer? Did you find the gun?"

"No, but I recognized his blue eyes. He's the guy in the cape I told you about."

"What? Are you back on that again?" Sheppard dug his heels into the pavement, halting all forward movement. He pulled his arm from my grip. "You think you can identify a murderer solely on the color of his eyes?"

"And the scar over his brow." I resumed my hold on his arm and my tugging. Unfortunately this time, the inspector wasn't budging. "I know this is the guy I saw come out of the administration building. He has to have something to do with the murder. We just can't let him get away."

"The hell we can't." Sheppard pulled free for the second, and final time. "It may be perfectly fine for you to conjure up some supposition out of thin air and use it to magically catch a killer, but this isn't a movie. It's the real world and I need real facts to connect this guy to the crime."

"But Inspector—"

"Listen, you—" Now it was his turn to manhandle me. He grabbed hold of my cowboy vest and yanked me forward until we were only inches apart. "You may think you're some sort of big shot, but you're nothing special to me. You're nothing except Suspect Number One, and these pitiful attempts to mislead me aren't going to work. Lucky for you, I need facts too, otherwise you'd be wearing that little cowboy outfit behind bars." Sheppard let go so suddenly that my spurs played a disjointed tune as I struggled to keep my balance. "Be warned, Wainwright. I'm looking everywhere and when I find the facts, I'll take great pleasure watching you fry in the chair!"

He intimidated me with his cold, solemn stare. He was just trying to scare me, and he was doing a pretty good job. After a long moment, he swivelled around and stormed toward the parking lot.

While I didn't know Sheppard well, I strongly suspected he wasn't the type of man who would turn his back on someone he really thought was a murderer, even if he couldn't prove it. Hmm. If Sheppard didn't really think me guilty, then what was his problem?

Solving that mystery would have to wait for another day. I

had more pressing issues. Chad Harrington. Direct conversation and confrontation was unlikely to get me the facts I needed to convince Inspector Sheppard that Harrington was guilty. I would have to come up with another avenue of attack. And I knew just the place to start.

***

You wouldn't think a casting office could double for a junkyard, but ours certainly seemed to qualify. There was stuff everywhere. Most of the clutter was made up of piles and piles of actor head shots. Some were shoved into file folders, lying haphazardly on table tops and on every available chair, but most were on the floor, spread out in their own sort of photographic carpet. There were small paths where people could walk through, but they had to tread carefully. While a few were photos of more established talents, most were pictures of men and women, straight off busses coming from the Midwest and the South, each hoping to make it big in pictures. My photo had to be lying around there somewhere, a younger and perhaps a bit thinner version of myself.

I, of course, didn't arrive in Hollywood by bus. I came by train. Once peace had finally come to Europe, I wanted to get as far away from France as possible. Even the East Coast was too close, with only the Atlantic between me and the horror of my memories. So I got on a train heading west and went as far as I could, ending up in Hollywood. I was in town for less than a week before it dawned on me that the acting talents that had helped me survive my clandestine missions, could be put to a more entertaining and profitable use. Throw in a couple of connections from my army days, and a career was born.

A career suddenly sidetracked in the search for a murderer.

I carefully moved deeper into the room, avoiding the photos whenever I could. In addition to the pictures, the casting office was also a repository for hundreds of gifts, or bribes if you like, from the aforementioned wannabes. Each bribe was from someone hoping for a little more attention from the casting director. There was the obligatory candy, along with food stuffs of all kind. Some of it was so old, it was best not to look upon it too closely, lest you find some other form of life growing upon it. There were several bottles of alcohol, which would have been illegal to have in one's possession just a few years ago, and there was even a Victrola parked in the corner, though I couldn't imagine how it got there. The thing must have weighed a ton. The bribes were nice, if the intended recipient cared. Unfortunately for all the wannabes, our casting director didn't give a hoot for such stuff.

Timothy Edmunds did like cats though, which helped us become friends instantly, but for me was a double-edged sword. Sally was too swamped to cat-sit with all the sudden rewrites dumped on her, so yesterday I had left Penelope alone in my dressing room. When I returned hours later, I had found my favorite pillow shredded into pieces. Her statement of rebellion. Desperate, today I turned to Timothy for help, and now I was paying the price.

When I made it through the debris field, to the back of the room where Timothy's small desk and chair were situated, I saw a scandalous scene. There was my beloved Penelope, nestled quite comfortably in another man's lap. His fingers brushed back and forth across the fur of my baby. I wanted to punch him, but I tamped the urge down. I was here to ask a favor, not engage in a physical altercation.

Timothy knew me as well as I knew him. "Here you are,

come to take my companion away," he said as he leaned forward to hand Penelope over to me.

I cradled my princess in my arms, stroking her lovingly. "Go get one of your own," I countered, confident now that my baby was mine once again. My comment was silly, as I intended it to be. I knew full well Timothy had several cats at home and a couple of dogs too. "Thanks for looking after her for me," I added. "I didn't dare leave her alone again."

"As always, it's my pleasure, but why are you even here? Aren't you on hiatus for the rest of the week?"

"I'm doing a little extra curricular activity, and I need your help."

"Anything."

I carefully deposited Penelope on the desktop, while I moved a stack of papers from a nearby chair to the floor. I reached for my baby once again and sat, settling her in my lap. "I met a guy on the cowboy set today. He's only an extra but I need to know more about him and I was hoping you would have his address."

"That's no problem. What's his name?"

"Chad Harrington."

"Hmm. Chad Harrington, Harrington." Timothy got up, headed toward a stack to the right, and rifled through file folders. He didn't have a secretary, or a filing system as far as I could see, but that never seemed to hamper him much. "Tall, skinny guy, blond, blue eyes, scar over the left brow, totally full of himself?"

"That's him," I said, amazed once again. "Out of the hundreds of guys who come through here every week, how do you remember them all?"

"I don't exactly, I'll confess, but this guy stood out."

"How so?"

Timothy had finished with the first stack, apparently finding nothing, and then picked up the next one. "He didn't come bearing gifts like most of the others. Seemed to think the world was his oyster, and I should automatically give him the lead role in our best picture just because he was so wonderful."

"Why give such a jerk any part at all? Why not just boot his sorry ass right off the lot?"

"Two reasons, I suppose. One was he was becoming such an annoyance, he wouldn't have left without a major fuss, and I wasn't in the mood to deal with him. Second, the director of the singing cowboy film had just rung me up, bitching about the quality of the extras I had been sending him, so I decided to give him Harrington as a token of my love."

We shared a delightfully wicked smile. "Remind me to not get on your bad side."

"As long as you take care of your Penelope, you will always stay on my good side."

I gave my princess a pat and she snuggled a bit closer. "No worries there."

Timothy finished with the second stack, and moved onto a third. Halfway down, he found success. "Ah." He opened the folder and handed the photo to me. "Is this is the guy?"

One look and I was sure. Even though the picture was black and white, the intensity within his gaze was the same. This was not only the man I had met in the commissary, he was the man I met in front of the administration building. "That's him."

"Okay. His address is written down on the back."

I flipped over the photo and saw it was an address on somewhere on Sunset. I reached forward for a pen, jostling Penelope in the process. She howled and I froze. The death claws were out.

Timothy laughed. "Don't move", he said. "I'll do it."

I wasn't sure if I should be pleased by his offer, or mortified that he knew I was such a wimp when it came to dealing with my cat. I decided to go with the former rather than the latter. "Thanks."

"You're always so entertaining Theodore," Timothy said as he copied down the information.

I thanked him for his trouble. Draping Penelope over my shoulders, I left with Harrington's address in hand. Time to unmask this caped crusader once and for all, and show the world who he really was.

CHAPTER FOUR

Though I had given Sally a sandwich a few hours ago, and she'd promised me she would eat it, I didn't believe her. I checked my watch. It was half-past two. No point in dragging Sally away from her typewriter now. The Brown Derby—a real restaurant with hearty meals, not just sandwiches—wouldn't open for dinner service for another hour and a half. So I had plenty of time to make a little excursion to Sunset Boulevard.

"Ready for a little ride, my princess?" I asked Penelope.

She shifted a little around my neck, as she lifted her head. She was not fond of riding in my roadster, but I was hopeful she would tolerate it. We had spent so little time together in recent days, perhaps her desire to be with me would outweigh her dislike of automobile travel.

Five minutes later, after checking the address that Timothy had written down for me, I was in my car and heading down Sunset Boulevard. It wasn't too bad. Penelope complained heartily for a few minutes, and then she settled down for a nap. Relieved, I spent the rest of the drive wondering what kind of place Chad Harrington would chose to call home. I didn't expect to learn much, but perhaps by taking a quick peek at the exterior, I might gain insight into the man who dwelled within. Harrington's address was somewhere near Sunset and Vermont, not the spiffiest neighborhood in Hollywood. Shoving the address back into my pocket, I wondered briefly if Harrington was a single-family home sort of man, complete with a wife and 2.3 children, but somehow I doubted that. Harrington just didn't seem the type who could share his attention with other people.

When I arrived, I discovered my theory was correct. Harrington lived in the Imperial Palms Residential Hotel. A grand name for not such a grand location. It was, in fact, a dump. The type of place where a man down on his luck, but with a few dollars in his pocket, could stay and at least have a roof over his head, and a lumpy mattress to sleep on.

Being an extra in the motion picture business was not the most lucrative endeavor, but I suspected Harrington wanted fame more than money, and right now he had neither. So how could Montgomery's murder change that situation? The motive behind the crime still seemed murky to me. Perhaps it would become clearer with time. I was disappointed as I pulled away, and headed back towards the studio, since my questions weren't magically answered just by looking at the outside of Harrington's residence.

An idea struck me. It was a wild idea, but it was a good way forward. "Penelope my love, this may have not been a wasted drive after all." She didn't respond to my voice, but when I started to whistle, she yowled to accompany me. I was happy. I had a plan.

***

Sally was right where I expected her to be, chained to her desk. What I hadn't expected was to find her sound asleep at four in the afternoon. She was using a pile of scripts as a make shift pillow, and even in her sleep Sally looked worn. In the nearly twenty years since we'd first met, I had never known her to be out in public unless she was impeccably dressed and she never, ever let anyone see her looking weak. This was a profoundly disturbing development.

Drat it all.

There was no sign of Spencer. He probably went out to enjoy a liquid lunch again, leaving Sally behind to do all the heavy lifting, so to speak. She had tried to warn me that her work-load was too much, but I was too busy playing detective to listen. Something had to be done.

I carefully removed Penelope from my neck, letting her curl up among the piles of paper, and I shook Sally's shoulder hard. "Sally, wake up."

"Wha?"

"Come on, Sally. Wake up."

She blinked, and it was a few moments before awareness fully returned to her. "Oh Teddy. What time is it?"

"Five o'clock will be arriving shortly."

"Oh dear." She fumbled around, struggling to establish some sort of order in her workspace. "I promised myself I would only close my eyes for a moment, and here I've slept for over an hour."

"Only an hour?" I slid a finger under her chin and forced her to look up at me. "It seems like you need much more than an hour's sleep. Did you even go home last night?" Her guilty flush was answer enough. "Oh, Sally."

"Well, what do you expect?" She waved her hand over a pile of scripts, before snatching one at random and shoving it at me. "Farnsworth has gone through every single one of them, and is demanding major changes in them all!"

I flipped through the pages and saw scribbles made by a red pen, filling up nearly every page. "What kind of changes?"

"It isn't just removing profanity, or taking out any gratuitous sex, that's obvious. Farnsworth wants to change characters, or rewrite scenes to make sure that no one in a story does anything slightly immoral, has any impure thoughts, or has any sympathies toward the criminal element." In other words taking out anything that was interesting about what it was to be a human being. Sally went on. "We can't show men and women in bed together, even if they are married. That would be far too scandalous."

"Now you're being silly."

"Not me, Farnsworth," she countered. "Here's the list of do's and don'ts he gave us yesterday."

She handed me a stack of paper which I perused through with growing dismay. I couldn't believe it. "This thing is ten pages long," I said. Now I was beginning to understand why Sally looked so frazzled.

She took the papers back, and flipped through them. About six pages in, she removed a sheet and handed it to me. "This is my favorite one."

I read a paragraph, blinked, then read it again. The unbelievable print hadn't changed. "They actually think someone could learn how to dynamite a train or crack a safe by watching a movie?"

She nodded, leaning back to quote the rule, which she had apparently memorized. "While writing such scenes, one should have in mind the effect in which descriptions of too much detail may have upon the moron!"

Astounding. "Farnsworth may call himself the Paragon of

JULIE B. BRAYTON

Virtue, but it sounds to me like he's the one who is the moron."

"Maybe so, Teddy, but ever since Mr. Montgomery's death, Mr. Owens has let Farnsworth have full run of the script department, with absolutely dreadful results."

I picked up a script at random and began to read. Dreadful indeed. Despite Sally's excellent skills as a writer, the scene laid out before me was stripped of all joy and all life. Any signs of adult interaction or any human interaction at all had been completely sanitized away. Even the best actor in the world wouldn't be able to do much with this bland soda cracker.

I thought back to the divorcee picture of the other day. That production couldn't be watered down. I wondered if it was going to be shelved. I didn't really care about that movie, but something tugged at the back of my brain. Something was bothering me about this script. Something other than the type written on the page. Despite my best efforts, nothing surged forward, so I tossed the script back onto the pile. "What I can't understand is why this is happening all at once. Other studios have been operating under censorship for a few years. Why were we not forced to work under the code until now?"

"R.K. must have been able to keep the lions at bay."

I thought back to the letter he dictated in his office, where I overheard the strength of his character first hand. "He was not one to be trifled with."

"Now that he's gone, this entire backlog must be dealt with at once."

"Not at once." Determined, I pulled Sally to her feet and handed over her coat. "You have been working far too long, and far too hard, young lady. Right now I am taking you out for a fine dinner at the Brown Derby, and then you are heading home to get some proper rest."

"Oh, Teddy, I can't." She tugged out of her coat and out of

my arm at the same time. "Mr. Farnsworth will be here any second demanding a progress report."

"Farnsworth can go to hell!"

"How dare you sir!"

The voice came from the doorway behind me. I had never heard it before, but there was no doubt in my mind to whom it belonged. I turned and found Farnsworth, all prim and proper in an impeccably tailored tweed suit, holding his hat in his hand. The round shape of his glasses couldn't hide his beady eyes, or the shark-like aspects of his demeanor.

Paragon of Virtue, my ass.

"No, sir," I countered, not giving any ground. "How dare you? How dare you treat people like your own personal slaves."

"You... you can't speak to me this way," Farnsworth stammered. "Don't you know who I am?"

I shoved my hands in my pockets. I wanted to show him that he couldn't intimidate me. "I know, sir, that you claim to be the guardian of all things good and decent here in Hollywood, but that claim is obviously false if you have it in your nature to work other good people to an early death."

"Now, you see here, young man." Apparently I had hit a nerve. "You think I don't recognize you, but I do. You're the star of those two-bit detective dreadfuls."

"Detective Tompkins is worth a dollar, if he's worth anything."

Farnsworth wasn't impressed. "This studio has been putting out scandalous and shameful productions for far too long, I tell you, and it's high time these sinful practices are stopped."

"Why is that?"

"Why is what?" Farnsworth asked, thrown off by my question.

"Why have we been able to produce such scandalous materials for so long? Why haven't you been on the lot before now?"

The only sound that came from Farnsworth was violent, noisy breathing. This went on for almost a minute, and I became concerned when Farnsworth started to shake. I braced myself for anything, including a physical attack. No attack came, at least not a physical one, and finally Farnsworth found his voice. "That is immaterial. What is important is that these story lines must be corrected, immediately."

"Not at the expense of this woman's health. How do you think the press would react if they learned that Hollywood's Paragon of Virtue was willing to work people to death, like he was running his very own sweat-shop? Now there's a story that would grab headlines nationwide." And it would. There was nothing people liked better than to read some juicy scandal, or laugh at a great, big hypocrite over their morning coffee.

"You are one to talk of headlines," he spat.

Despite my current sensationalism, it didn't make my threat any less potent. Farnsworth saw that and he didn't like it. He was a bully, wrapped up in a deceptive blanket of decency, used to being the one who dished out the threats, not being forced to endure them. He clenched his fists, and then as stiff as a wooden board, he bowed toward Sally. "My apologies, Miss Jones. In my excitement to improve the quality of films produced at RKM Studios, I simply did not see the toll this was taking on you and your coworkers."

Surprised, Sally fumbled for a moment, and then her instincts of politeness and good grace kicked in. "Apology accepted, Mr. Farnsworth."

"I believe enough work has been done for the moment, and we can begin shooting some of the rewritten scenes tomorrow. Why don't you leave now and take the rest of the day off. This way, you can be sharp when you return to your typewriter in the morning."

"Thank you, Mr. Farnsworth."

Farnsworth bowed once again, and was about to leave when my voice stopped him. "Since when do you determine shooting schedules around here?"

He looked at me, his eyes hard and cold. "Since Mr. Montgomery met his maker. There is a new administration now. No more films will be released from this studio unless they meet the high standards of the decency code, and with the deplorable state of production at RKM, this means certain scenes in every production will need to be shot again. Including films that have been previously completed, but not yet released. Those have priority."

What the hell? "You don't have the right to make those decisions? You're not the head of this studio."

"Oh? Check with Owens if you have any doubts. The acting head of RKM has given me full reign." Farnsworth took a step toward me. "I would be careful, Mr. Wainwright. I do not approve of your association with this sordid murder, and I don't approve of you. I am taking a very close look at the storyline for your next *Detective Tompkins* mystery, and if it is not up to snuff, and if you are not up to snuff, you will be gone. Beware of me, Mr. Wainwright."

"I will, but you beware of me too, Mr. Paragon of Virtue!" I pulled my hand out of my pocket and jabbed a finger at his chest. He wasn't the only one who could talk tough.

He held my stare for a moment longer, and then left the room.

I allowed the bad feeling in the air to dissipate, before addressing Sally. "Well, since you are now awake, and free, let us head to my roadster and to the Brown Derby where I have already made dinner reservations."

Sally was not mollified by my attempt at normalcy. "Teddy, he just threatened to fire you."

"I know." I held up her coat, but she made no move to put it on.

"Farnsworth doesn't care if you are the biggest moneymaker on the lot. I get the feeling he'd happily let RKM go under if he thought it would teach you a lesson."

"No worries. I won't let that happen." I tried to sound calm, but deep down I was beginning to feel concerned. Not for myself. Thanks to Detective Tompkins, I had made enough money to last several lifetimes, but I was worried about everyone else on the lot. I would have to find a way to ensure their safety.

A glance at the clock showed it was now nearing five. We were late. I shook her coat. "Come on now. Despite my power is a movie star, they won't hold our table forever."

"All right." Sally knew darn well I was blustering, but she let it go for the moment.

Properly arrayed with outer coats, and hats upon our heads, and my cat around my neck, we headed out the door. "I have some news to tell you about R.K.'s case while we eat and I desperately need your stellar advice about my next course of action."

"Teddy, what trouble are you getting into now?"

I smiled at her, a smile she knew full well meant lots and lots of trouble. "You will see."

***

"Theodore I have said it before and I will say it again, you are an idiot."

"Yes, Sally," I sighed. "I will have to agree with you this time."

When I had made my reservation at the Brown Derby earlier over the phone, I had forgotten that I was supposedly trying to keep a low profile. The press and the gossip queens alike were on the lookout for me all over the city, and here I wanted to eat in the middle of the gossip center that is Hollywood. It had only been open for a few years, but in that time, the Brown Derby had become the place to see and to be seen, especially when it came to industry types. Sally suggested we dine elsewhere, but I refused. I was getting tired of being pushed around by events that weren't my fault.

Still, I had a bit of common sense left. I swung the roadster by my hotel to drop off Penelope and pay a bellhop to look after her, as some restaurants did not welcome a cat in their dining room, no matter how well-behaved the feline was. She had forgiven me for abandoning her earlier with Timothy, and with the bribe of a can of tuna, she was content to remain in the bellhop's care for the time being. While I was there, I took the opportunity to ring up the maître d' on the phone. After a hasty consultation, he assured me there would be a secluded booth in the back waiting for me when I arrived. Slightly mollified, Sally held her tongue, for the rest of the drive to the restaurant.

I parked in the alley behind the restaurant, where the maître d' and a valet were waiting for us. I handed the keys to the valet, and then the maître d' escorted us inside. The afore-promised secluded booth was indeed there, and Sally and I settled in to peruse the menu.

"What looks good," I asked her, knowing full well she was eyeing the prices rather than the food. "Dinner is on me. We've been through a hell of a week so far, we deserve one chance to enjoy ourselves." Sally opened her mouth to protest, to show that independent streak of hers once again, but I spoke quickly before she had the chance. "Not this time, my dear Sally, I am paying and that is that. For once don't worry about how much it costs, and enjoy the moment."

She closed her mouth, and gave me the strangest look, one I've never seen from her before: a mixture of exasperation, and compassion. "Very well," she conceded. "Just this once."

"Thank you." Relaxing, I returned my attention to the menu. "So as I was asking, what looks good?"

"Perhaps the lobster," she said, with a twinkle in her eyes. It was the most expensive item on the menu, and I knew she was testing my boundaries.

"Lobster it is then," I assured her before she could protest. "And I will have the fillet mignon."

Realizing she had been outmaneuvered, Sally took her defeat with the good grace she always had, and politely put aside her menu.

Our waiter must've been waiting just out of sight, because he appeared immediately. I gave him our order, along with a request for an excellent matching wine. Then he left us to chat while our food was being prepared.

"So," Sally said, in a soft voice to make sure we were not over-heard. "You mentioned something about Mr. Montgomery's murder?"

"Yes," I said, excited. "The man in the cape, I found him." I told her about how I had uncovered Chad Harrington's identity. "I even drove by his hotel earlier, to give the place a look over."

"Where is it?"

"In a part of Hollywood that is, shall we say, less then ex-quisite." I reached in my pocket and all I felt was material. "Drat it."

"What's the matter?"

"I lost the paper with the address to the residential hotel. It must have fallen out of my pocket at some point."

"So? You're not planning on moving in are you?"

A tiny smile quirked my lips. "I am, sort of."

Sally leaned back in her chair and crossed her arms. "Theodore, what are you getting yourself into now?"

I smiled widely. Was there anyone on else on the planet who knew me as well as Sally did? "When I saw what a shoddy place the Imperial Palms really was, it gave me an idea—what?"

Sally uncrossed her arms, leaned forward and grasped my hands. "You're so sure it's him," she asked. "That Harrington is the man you saw?"

I thought back to those eyes. "I'm sure."

"But how can you be?" Sally tugged my hands a fraction closer to her side of the table. "Youre putting yourself at risk, Teddy. He could cause a lot of trouble for you if you're wrong. Is it worth it?"

I wanted to blurt out *yes*, but then I forced myself to take a step back. Was I sure? Yes, yes I was. But I hadn't seen the caped crusader's face, and blue eyes were blue eyes. What made his so different? It wasn't the eye color: it was the intensity. They made me feel uncomfortable: they made me feel like the mind behind them wasn't totally normal. I couldn't explain it, but I believed it. Believed it enough to keep going.

"Sally," I patted her hand. "I am sure he's the one, and yes, it is worth the risk."

She held my gaze for a moment more, and then looked away, instantly breaking the tension that I had only just realized was there. "All right, then," she said as she leaned back, reaching for her wine glass. "What is your next step?"

"I need proof. Proof strong enough to take to Sheppard, and

the only place I'm likely to find it is inside Harrington's home."

"So, how exactly do you plan to get inside?"

I was about to answer when the waiter arrived with our meal. We waited politely while he deposited the plates before us and refilled our wine glasses. After he was done, I raised my glass in a toast for luck, and explained my idea.

***

The screwdriver slipped from my butterfingers again, gouging a chunk of skin from my index finger. Drat it! I stuck the finger in my mouth to staunch the flow, and then risked a look around the lobby.

There were a few armchairs scattered around the not-so-grand entrance way of the Imperial Palms Residential Hotel. None of them were in good shape, which matched the condition of most of the men sitting in them. One was reading a paper two days old, two others were napping, or more likely sleeping it off. There was one guy walking across the lobby who couldn't be missed, however. I was told his name was Watkins, and he weighed three hundred pounds, despite the depression. I wondered how he ate so well during these hard times, and then decided it was none of my business. I was here for a different purpose.

No one seemed to have noticed my little accident, which was all I cared about for the moment. I picked up the screwdriver, and then glanced at the library book on easy furniture repair lying on the floor at my side. You wouldn't think attaching a leg to an end table would be so hard, but it was turning out to be one of the most challenging things I had ever done. I had a good excuse, of course. There wasn't much call for woodworking skills from the star on a movie set. Still,

I had to get the hang of it quick, or my new career as a hotel handyman was going to be short lived.

First thing that morning I had appeared in the hotel lobby wearing grimy overalls. My hair was tucked under a workman's cap, my eyes were hidden behind thick glasses, and my nose was lengthened just a bit, thanks to some theatrical putty. I had offered my skills as a multi-talented repair man. Since I was offering to work for no wages, giving the impression I was simply grateful for a roof over my head, as so many poor souls during these hard times were, my application was cheerfully accepted. Once gainfully employed, so to speak, I did a quick reconnaissance of the place and found that Harrington had rented a room on the second floor, Room 21B to be exact.

Now this was a room I very much wanted to inspect, and I would have my chance soon. Just before I became a handyman, I'd called up Timothy and asked for a very big favor. It was a favor that would cost me sometime in the future, but that would be a price I would gratefully pay if my work today was successful.

I checked my pocket watch. Half-past noon. Hmmm. Timothy should have come through for me by now. I fiddled with the table leg. Perhaps when acting opportunities dried up, I would take the skills I was learning today and carve out a new career, so to speak. I could picture it clearly, having a little shop of my own some day. Idling away the hours, polishing the same, simple piece of wood over and over. No worries, no pressure, no money coming from selling no furniture. Dying of starvation, only to end up buried in one of my own caskets—

There went my imagination again, taking over when I needed to keep my mind on business. Speaking of business, where the hell was Harrington? I couldn't stay here for too much longer without attracting attention, a situation that became even more dire when I looked down and saw that I had actually fixed the damn table. I hadn't really wanted to repair the leg. It was just an excuse to hang around the lobby until Harrington came out, but here it was, good as new, whether I wanted it to be or not. Drat it.

I hastily unscrewed the leg so I could start fixing it again, trying to be as patient as I could. I had asked Timothy to call Harrington precisely at noon and tell him that he was needed at the studio immediately. A new and exciting role had just come up, one Harrington would be perfect for. It should've been too much of a lure for Harrington to resist, yet here it was, half-past noon, and there was still no sign of him on the threadbare steps. The pass key I had purloined from the maid's cart was resting in my pocket and weighing heavy against my hip. Would I ever get the chance to use it?

"Hey, Jenkins," the desk clerk called. "Aren't you finished with that table yet?"

It took me a second to realize he was talking to me. I'd forgotten that Jenkins was my new name. "Almost sir."

"Well, hurry it up."

"Yes sir."

The clerk grumbled while he returned to his paper. The way he'd been attached to that chair all day, I was wouldn't have thought he would notice me at all. Still, it was a sign. My time skulking about the lobby was growing short.

A creak from the well-used stair caught my attention. Finally. There was Harrington, in his splendor, coming down to the lobby. He didn't so much as spare a glance for anyone else in the room before he was through the front door and gone. I waited an extra minute or so, to make good and sure that he wouldn't suddenly change his mind and return, and then gathered my toolbox and headed for the stairs. Now was my chance.

Have screwdriver will travel, I thought as I carried it proudly in my left hand, the tool-box clenched in my right, looking every inch like the handyman I had now become. A handyman who had every right to skulk—I mean, *stride*—down the second floor corridor toward Harrington's door. This was acting! I was thrilled with my performance, but I should have saved my major acting ability. The hallway was empty. Oh well. The performer in me was disappointed, but perhaps it was for the best. Since I was about to commit the crime of breaking and entering, it was better to not be observed in the process.

I reached Harrington's door, and with a deft twist of my purloined passkey, I was in. His room was like most rooms the Imperial Palms had to offer. They all had a small living area and even smaller bedroom. No kitchen, of course, just a hot plate. Bathroom facilities were shared down the hall. Small, cheap, and shabby, just like the rest of this dump. The walls were covered with wallpaper so old that some of the flowers were almost completely faded. Thirteen mirrors hung strategically around the room. Obviously this guy wasn't superstitious. There were also plenty of framed photographs, but they didn't hold images of pretty girls. They were all pictures of Harrington. Everywhere he looked when he was home, he saw himself. Amazing.

One other thing on the end table caught my attention: a paper pamphlet for a plastic surgeon in Beverly Hills. I picked it up. Now why in the world would Harrington want something like that? Considering where he lived, I seriously doubted he had sufficient funds to pay for a plastic surgeon, and why would such a vain person like Harrington consider such surgery? Surely a man with mirrors all over the place considered his image to be perfect.

But his face wasn't perfect. It was marred by that scar over his eyebrow. Harrington would obsess about it until it was gone, but there would be no way to remove it until he came up with some serious money. Was in Montgomery's murder a way for him to get money? I didn't immediately see how that would be the case, but I was still missing some of the pieces to the puzzle. It was time to look around some for some more of those pieces. Hopefully I would find something that would tie Harrington to Montgomery's death.

It turned out there wasn't much to go through. Harrington didn't seem to own many possessions other than photographs and mirrors. Not altogether surprising, given the rough economic climate. I thought he would have at least a radio in the corner, or a phonograph.

A pile of scripts lay scattered on the table and I flipped through them, wondering why Harrington had them in his possession. I didn't recall seeing him in any of those pictures. Most of the screenplays were unmarked, but there were some changes in red and blue ink here and there. Some lines were circled. They must have been movies where Harrington actually said a word or two on camera. A step up from an extra, but hardly nearing stardom.

I found nothing else of interest in the living room, so went to check out the bedroom, such as it was. It held a small bed and an even smaller closet. It was the closet where most of Harrington's income had to have gone. It was full of designer suits and expensive shirts. Of course, Harrington would only dress in the best. It wouldn't do for him to show himself off in anything less. I picked up one of the hats to see if it really was a Homburg, which sold for a whopping $3.99 downtown.

It was, but that wasn't the most important thing. The most important thing was resting underneath it.

Sitting on wooden shelf, poorly hidden under the hat, was a pistol. I knew better than to touch it, but I risked a small step forward and saw it was the same caliber that killed Montgomery. Had I found the murder weapon?

I couldn't be sure, of course, but at least I had a fact I could use to convince Detective Sheppard that Harrington was indeed a suspect. I put the hat back where I'd found it and was about to leave when the front door flew open.

"What are you doing in here?"

Drat it. Harrington came back early, and he looked mad enough to kill.

"Sir." I was in trouble now. "The sink was backing up. I came to fix."

"Crap!" He pointed a shaking finger at me. "I saw you slinking up the stairs. You're here to rob me."

What? "No, sir," I protested feebly. Even if I were a thief, what in the world would I take? There was nothing worthwhile in that dump except for his clothes.

Facts didn't seem to register with Harrington, who was so furious he was rembling. He was radiating enough rage that I began to wonder, was I looking into the eyes of a killer? Did Harrington have another weapon on him? Was he going to shoot me where I stood?

He had no weapon. No bullets were fired. Instead, he ran into the hall. "Thief," he shouted. "Thief, help."

It was time to leave. As soon as his back was turned, I darted through the doorway, heading for the stairs. A heavy weight landed on my back, sending me crashing to the ground. I lay there, gasping for breath, being slowly crushed by Watkins, who had apparently come to the aid of his neighbor. A couple of other men filled the hall as the air was slowly squeezed from my chest.

Distant shouts from police reached my ears, and I knew then I was in for a fine pot of trouble.

***

I spent a quiet hour in lockup with twenty or so of my new best friends, trying to fight down the panic. It didn't work. The litany, "I've been arrested" circled around my head in an unbroken loop.

Of course, having a behemoth who hadn't bathed in recent memory sitting next to me did not help. A tentative sniff found that most of the residents in the cell were in a similar condition. I couldn't tell what crimes they had committed simply by looking at them, and I surely wasn't going to ask, but I could make some educated guesses. Most were drunkards, which came as no surprise. No matter how down on their luck most men had become, they always seemed to come up with enough money for a drink.

When I smelled a whiff of alcohol on the behemoth's breath I relaxed slightly. Perhaps he wasn't a crazed killer, just a drunkard. I wasn't so confident about some of the others. Nor was I confident that I wouldn't be spending more time with them behind bars. Perhaps years.

Arrested.

For burglary.

I panicked, envisioning a future time, perhaps twenty years from now, walking free from the prison where I had served my term. An older, yet no less beautiful, Sally would be there to greet me, holding a photo of my dearly departed Penelope. Oh, Penelope. As much as Sally cared for her, Sally would never share her caviar tidbits with my beloved as I did. Or perhaps I would die behind bars, stabbed with a shank made out of a butter knife and tin foil. Perhaps I wouldn't even live to see tomorrow. Perhaps the behemoth next to me would strangle the life out of me with his bare hands.

I tensed, shutting my eyes while I waited for the end. As the minutes passed and no end came, I began to relax. There was no strangulation by the behemoth, no dismemberment, or any notice given by anyone else in the cell. I slapped the back of my hand. There went my vivid imagination again. Unchecked, it became a bother at times. I was going to have to work to control it in the future. And I would have a future, I saw that now.

I was in a unique situation, far different than anyone else in the cell. I, Theodore Wainwright, star of the *Detective Tompkins* movies, one of the most popular film series on the silver screen today, hadn't been arrested. Jenkins the handyman at the Imperial Palms Hotel had been arrested. My recently slapped hand touched my face. I wanted proof my disguise was still intact, but wiggling around the nose putty could draw the very attention I dared not seek. I forced myself to sit calmly. Breathing was somewhat restricted through the fake nose, so the prosthetic must've still been in place. My hair was still washed through with the Henna rinse and my overalls were still greasy and stained. Yes, I was still Jenkins the handyman, and as long as I could hang onto that persona I had the advantage.

An hour passed, then two. I had gotten so comfortable I didn't react when a copper called out my name. He was shouting for Jenkins, after all. My brain woke up and I struggled to my feet.

"Here." The copper gestured to the door. An invitation that

I gratefully accepted. I staggered out of the cell and came face to face with Harrington, who looked so anxious, I was afraid he might explode.

"This the guy?" The copper gestured toward me.

"Yes, Officer. I caught him inside my apartment. Obviously he was trying to steal my valuables."

"What valuables?" I didn't mean to blurt it out. I hadn't meant to say anything at all, but I couldn't help it. "There's nothing of value in that dump."

"Nothing of value?" Harrington gasped. "What about my photographs?"

"Photographs?"

"You mean you had some expensive pictures in your room?" the copper asked. "Taken by some hotshot photographer, like that Yosemite guy?"

I didn't remember seeing anything expensive in Harrington's room. Harrington seemed to be just as thrown by the question. "What? No. Who would ever want something like that? I'm talking about photos of me."

"Of you?"

Obviously the copper had thought he was speaking to a rational human being. Now he was beginning to learn differently. There seemed to be no end to the depths of Harrington's egotism.

The copper latched onto Harrington's sleeve. "You mean to tell me we had this poor fella hauled all the way down here cause you were afraid he was gonna steal pictures of you?"

"Of course." Harrington sounded so matter-of-fact. "All it takes is one glance and any young woman instantly falls in love with me. They would pay any amount to have a photo of me as a keepsake, especially one from my very own hotel room."

"Uh huh."

The appreciation of all things "Harrington" didn't seem to extend to the copper, who was getting more and more annoyed. He turned toward me. "I'm sorry, fella. I didn't realize we was dealing with a loony here." Harrington squawked, but the copper ignored him. "You're free to go."

What a relief. "Thank you, Officer." I left Harrington to express his complaints to the copper and got out of there quickly.

My near miss with permanent incarceration made me realize I was getting in over my head here. Sheppard was going to have to listen to me now, whether he liked it or not.

I walked down the front steps of the precinct and onto the street. Some uniformed officers were bringing in another suspect up the stairs. A young man and his lady were walking toward the park across the street. Another man, dressed in overalls pushed a wide broom down the sidewalk. It didn't seem like anyone was paying attention to me. The trouble was, I didn't want to leave. I urgently needed to speak to Inspector Sheppard, but if the copper I just left saw Jenkins the handyman again it would raise some unwelcome questions.

I couldn't go home to change. My Hollywood apartment was half an hour away by cab, and forty-five minutes by trolley. It would take far too long, and I had to tell Inspector Sheppard about the gun on Harrington's shelf. I would have to risk going back inside as Jenkins, and just hope the copper wouldn't catch sight of me.

I turned to go back up the steps, when a man brushed by me. I climbed upward for a step or two more before I realized I had nearly made a mistake. That had been Sheppard, walking right past me, and I hadn't even noticed. By the time my brain woke up, he was halfway across the street, heading for a hot dog stand in the park.

Lunch time. Sheppard gave a dime to the vendor and took his hot dog, which was buried under a stack of sauerkraut, and his root beer to a park bench with a good view of the pigeons. I crossed the street and carefully approached the bench, hat in hand.

"No, handouts today," Sheppard muttered between bites.

I was impressed. He didn't act like he had noticed me at all, but apparently he had. "Excuse me, Inspector Sheppard," I let my cultured voice come through, in sharp contrast to my roughened exterior, "but I'm not looking for a handout. I need your help."

Sheppard's mouth flew open and he nearly dropped his hot dog. He narrowed his eyes as he leaned forward for a better look. "Wainwright? Are you hiding behind that Gawd-awful nose?"

"Very good, Inspector," I sat next to him and stretched, enjoying the fresh air after being locked up for so long.

"What are you doing here, and wearing coveralls? You look like a bum."

"I'm not a bum. I am a handyman."

What Sheppard thought of my proclamation I will never know, but I didn't give him time to ponder about nonessentials. I quickly described my morning and as I talked, my unease grew. Sheppard was still as a stone, letting his hot dog cool, looking only straight ahead. When I told him about the gun in Harrington's closet, he jumped to his feet, not caring when his hot dog tumbled into the dirt, and grabbed me by the lapels. He hauled me to my feet and held my face inches away from his. "You are under arrest."

"You can't be serious." While I fully expected the anger, I hadn't expected this. "For what?"

"Withholding evidence."

"You're being absurd. I was going to come to you as soon as I found the gun, then I was delayed by my ridiculous arrest."

"I'm not talking about the gun, I'm talking about Harrington. You should have come to me the moment you recognized him."

"I did tell you." I pushed myself away from him, trying to reestablish some space between us, and some dominance. "We had a conversation while I was in a cowboy suit, which I'm sure you remember very well. You said you needed facts before you could do anything, then you walked away from me, leaving me on my own. So that's what I did. I acted on my own."

"Oh." I had cornered Sheppard with logic. Some men, when caught in an embarrassing moment, would get even angrier, furious when someone pointed out his mistake. Fortunately Sheppard wasn't such a man. All of the bluster left him in a rush, and he sat heavily back onto the bench. "You're right. I didn't take your concerns seriously. I'm sorry."

"Thank you," I said quietly, sitting next to him. I should have let it go. I had told Sheppard about the gun. My obligations were now finished. Common sense told me to get up, kindly thank the inspector for his time, and depart. I didn't. I was curious about the man sitting next to me, and sometimes when I'm curious, common sense gets thrown out the window. "Why don't you like me?"

Sheppard remained silent for a long time. I was afraid I had angered him again. "Because, I'm not an idiot."

"What?"

"I'm not an idiot," he repeated, hopping off of the bench once more. Suddenly the calm and cool detective was replaced by an impassioned man. "The police in your movies are all bumbling fools. They trip over suspects, accidentally destroy evidence, and are never smart enough to catch a killer."

He was angry about my movies? I wasn't expecting this. Of course Detective Tompkins had to be smarter than the police. He was the lead character, he had to be the one to solve the crime, but in the years I had been playing an on-screen investigator, I had never considered the impact my films had on real policemen. Sheppard certainly seemed to be offended.

"Don't you see, we're not like that at all," the inspector said. "Police officers are intrepid and strong and smart. If we were really like the idiots in your movies, no crimes would ever get solved. "He touched my arm in what I would have called an imploring gesture, if I were a dramatist. "Why can't you show us how we really are in your pictures?"

I didn't answer immediately. Sheppard had asked a serious question, and he deserved a serious and thoughtful reply. Now I understood why he had been so angry with me. He thought I was denigrating his profession, and perhaps in a way my films were, but they had a different purpose. A purpose that could be difficult to explain to the policeman, but I had to try. "How do you relax, Inspector Sheppard?"

"What?" He seemed thrown by my unexpected question. "Are you trying to dodge the subject?"

"No," I insisted, shifting closer, intent on making my point. "Do you read more crime reports? Sharpen up your fingerprinting skills? Polish your gun? Do you think about you work constantly?"

"Of course not. Working all the time would drive a man crazy." He hesitated for a moment, perhaps deciding how much personal information he truly wanted to share with me. "I do putter around in the garden a bit," he finally admitted.

"You spend time relaxing in your garden, while others spend an afternoon relaxing inside a darkened movie house."

"I don't understand?"

"Everyone knows in real life policemen are competent people who should be respected, but I don't deal in real life."

"That's for sure."

Everybody's a critic. "Every day desperate people are working terribly hard to survive this horrible depression. It's a constant battle, and no one is strong enough to fight constantly. People need an escape, and my films provide an escape for some."

"I see your point, I really do, but I still don't understand why it has to come at the cost of my profession's reputation."

"If the police were to solve the crime in my films too easily then there is no mystery. People like playing detective along with me. They see the same clues, observe the same suspects, and try to see if they can discover the killer before I do. Then, if they're successful, they can return to those mean streets with their burden lightened just a little because they know they've accomplished something, even if it's only outwitting a celluloid detective."

Sheppard seemed to be giving my views serious consideration. "I suppose I never thought about it that way before."

"Everything is always tied up in a neat bow at the end of my pictures, with the killer conveniently confessing. It's a happy ending guaranteed, but this is real life. You have a chance now to catch a killer, to make sure there is, if not a happy ending, at least a satisfactory ending in the Montgomery murder case. Will you take it?"

I wondered if I had made my case, or destroyed it. I was just about to say something more when Sheppard released me. He adjusted his topcoat, tossed away his trash, and faced me while putting on his hat. "I suppose I could pay Mr. Harrington a little visit."

Thank goodness. We exchanged a nod, and then I watched

him walk briskly back toward the precinct. While I couldn't imagine that we would ever become friends, at least we were no longer enemies.

I reached up and removed that dratted putty from my face and gave my nose the healthy scratch it had wanted all day. Time to go home.

CHAPTER FIVE

I went back to the hotel to change and retrieve Penelope from the bellhop's care. Once again in my own clothes, and with a hearty room service meal inside me, I pondered my next step. I had done all I could to find Montgomery's killer, but now it seemed my time as an amateur sleuth was coming to an end. Now that Sheppard and I had cleared the air, I felt more comfortable about leaving the case in his competent hands.

Which meant, I supposed, I was finally and officially on vacation. I still had five days left before I was due to return to the *Detective Tompkins* set, and suddenly I had nothing to do with my time. Enjoying Sally's company was not an option. While she said her working hours had improved immensely, apparently I was persona non-grata at the writer's bungalow for the time being. With this destination temporarily removed, I was at loose ends. So now what?

I had originally planned to spend the week a few miles to the north. Like many of my fellow film stars, I had purchased an orchard in the San Fernando Valley. It was a good tax write off, and made for a nice getaway, when I could get there. It had a cozy ranch house, with a few acres of land for orange trees. Once a year I would hire some of the local men to pick the fruit and take it to market, making sure they received most of those profits. It wasn't much, but it was one way I could help out during this horrible depression. I had been looking forward to the solitude I would find there, before Montgomery's murder had sent my life tumbling topsy-turvy. Perhaps it was time to reinstate this plan.

With no official progress announced, and therefore no news, media interest in Montgomery's murder was dropping. The case had been relegated to the inside pages of the papers, and in what little coverage I could find, my name wasn't even mentioned. I called my caretaker at the orchard and was relieved to learn there hadn't been a sign of anyone from the fourth estate in over twenty four hours. Good. It was settled then. I would go home.

Driving to the valley wasn't like a simple drive around the park. The roads were, well, they weren't roads really. They were more like dirt ruts, kind of flattened out to pretend they were roads. If a lot of traffic traveled before me, the ruts would turn into gullies deep enough to destroy the undercarriage of the automobile. At other times, if it had rained, they would be full of mud. Little lakes of quicksand eager to latch onto the tires with an iron grip, dragging them down and preventing all forward movement. So no, one couldn't envision such a journey without making proper preparations.

I opened the trunk of my roadster and did a simple inventory, checking to make sure I had ample supplies of all my emergency equipment. Neatly arranged within was a bag of sand and a bag of gravel, and two or three wooden planks to get me out of the aforementioned ruts if the need arose. I also had a spare can of gasoline, several lanterns, extra food, water, and a first-aid kit. A couple of car rugs completed the necessities, and I was ready to undertake my fifteen mile trip to the valley.

I pressed the starter and the engine revved with a satisfying purr. There would be no purrs coming from my traveling companion however. With a little bit of effort, and only a couple of scratches, I was able to get Penelope inside her traveling crate. Although I'd filled it with her favorite blanket and toy to cuddle with, apparently she had had her fill of automobile travel in the last few days, and wasn't looking forward to more. For the first twenty minutes of our journey, all I got were complaints. I figured I had listened to about forty meows per mile. After a while, she settled down and reluctantly fell asleep. I knew she would be happy once we reached the ranch house.

I tried to drive smoothly to avoid jostling Penelope, but as we left the paved roads of the city, the challenge became more and more difficult.

The roadway was wet. It seemed it had rained in this area last night. Although there had been no precipitation in Beverly Hills, rain in Southern California was spotty at times. This was unwelcome news. Slowing down to a crawl, I kept a steady hand on the wheel. No speed records would be set today, but I was confident I would reach my destination intact.

I dodged two ruts, but wasn't quick enough to avoid a third. Those muddy quicksand-like fingers grabbed hold of my front right tire. The car lurched as it shuddered to a stop, waking Penelope, who began a new round of yowling.

Wonderful.

Like any fool, I tried to rev the engine a few times, but to no avail. There simply wasn't enough solid ground under the wheel for the tread to catch. Resigned to an immediate future of backbreaking effort, I got out and went to my emergency supplies in the trunk. I engaged in a bit of heavy lifting, removing the bags of sand and gravel, along with the wooden planks, and then set to work. I poured the sand into the hole, hoping it would absorb enough of the moisture from the mud so I could get the tire, and the car moving again, and then struggled to maneuver the planks into the proper position. I concentrated on two things: the task at hand and at keeping as much of the mud as possible off of my clothes.

Minutes passed before I realized that someone was behind me. Funny, I hadn't noticed anyone approaching. Even with all this mud muffling his footsteps, I thought I would have heard some noise. I was being silly. Who cared how he got here? I was stuck, and was grateful for the assistance. I stood up to thank him for his help, but before I could get out a word, or even get a glimpse of my benefactor, black gloved fingers slipped around my neck, closing in tight, strangling me.

I was being murdered.

I struggled every way I could to break free, latching my fingers around his arm to pull his hands away from my neck, but his grip was too strong. My fingers brushed some pieces of medal and I saw a flash of gold. What the heck was that? But I had no time for such frivolity.

I tossed from side to side to shake off my murderer, but the fellow had the grip of an ox. I tried to recall some of the self-defense training I had been given during the war, but my experience during those times was limited mainly to two areas, flinging myself daily to the bottom of a trench to avoid cannon fire, or using my theatrical skills to talk my way out of trouble. Neither was sufficient to help save me now. I couldn't even recall the judo tricks Sally's father had taught me when we were little. Desperate, I even tried something from one of my movies, suddenly lunging backwards, hoping to knock the killer off of his feet. He was ready for that maneuver too and stepped back just at the right time so I knocked myself off my feet, not him. With every passing moment I weakened just a bit, and with every passing moment the realization grew: I was about to die. There was nothing else I could do. I wasn't able to save myself.

My desperation turned into anger. How dare he? What gave him the right to take my life now, when so many Germans had failed on the battlefield? My indignation gave me strength, and I was able to pull his fingers away just enough to heave in one desperate gasp of air, but my opponent was desperate too. He had all the advantages. He tightened the grip to the utmost, going for the kill.

I made peace with the inevitable.

I heard the squeal of brakes, and shouts. At first I wasn't sure if the voices were real. Surely, I wouldn't imagine the scream of a young girl, even if I were near death?

The fingers around my throat lessened their grip, before the pressure disappeared entirely. I fell to my knees and gulped in air. The clamor of shouts and running footsteps surrounded me, but I had no energy to deal with such things. I could only concentrate on breathing. Oh, how nice it was to breathe. I sat in the mud, breathing, deciding that my clothes were now ruined and thrilled I was still around to be annoyed about that.

Words penetrated the roaring in my ears, a roaring I hadn't even aware of until just then. Someone was speaking to me, and had, in fact, been speaking to me for some time. I struggled to concentrate on the voice, and then a face swam into focus in front of me.

I blinked several times, for surely I was hallucinating. Was a young girl really crouched down next to me? She was, and she was talking, but the words made no sense.

Then I saw the book and the pen clutched in her hand. "You see, Mr. Wainwright, I simply am your biggest fan," she dithered on, oblivious that she had interrupted my murder. "May I have your autograph?"

***

"He was saved by a stalker?"

Was I really hearing voices next to me, or was I dreaming? My head was all in a muddle, and I hated muddle. Enough of this. I opened my eyes and found that I had somehow ended up in a hospital. I hoped it was a real hospital, and not some sort of medical set, but when I looked around I found there were four walls, so I supposed I was in the real thing. The main color theme of the room was white, of course. White sheets, white drapes on the window, a white pen with a matching notepad with a white cover, and even the pitcher and the glass on the table were white. At the foot of my bed was a nurse with a cap perched perfectly on top of her head. Her uniform was starch white as well, and she was chatting with Sally.

Sally. Dear, dear Sally. Her peacock-blue dress with matching bag was a welcome color contrast to the drabness of the rest of the place. She had deposited her small, round designer hat with a short veil attached to the brim on a nearby chair. With her face free of obstructions, I could clearly see that her eyes were somewhat puffy, with brown smudges beneath them. How long had she been here? How long had I been here?

"Sally," I said, relieved to find the word escaping my lips sounded fairly normal, despite that my throat hurt like the devil.

"Teddy." Sally moved to my side, her smile sending a twinkle to her eyes, removing the darkness that was there just an instant ago. She reached for my hand while the nurse headed toward the door.

"I'll inform the doctor," the nurse said, and left us alone.

"Sally, what happened—?" I was going to say more when a coughing fit overtook me.

"Relax, Teddy." She reached for the pitcher and poured water into the glass, and moved it close enough for me to sip. "Everything is fine now."

"Is it?" My current situation led me to think differently. Why couldn't I remember what happened? I vaguely recalled the presence of a young woman asking for my autograph, and then I was here. What happened while I was asleep? More importantly, what happened to Penelope?

I put the glass down with an alarming clank, not caring if it threatened to spill over, and struggled to get up. I heard Sally's commands for calm, but I ignored them. How could I have forgotten, even for a moment, about the well-being of one of the few creatures on Earth who loved me uncondition-ally, and who I loved back with equal fervor. I gripped Sally's arm. "Penelope? Where is she? Is she alright?"

The tight muscles in Sally's arm relaxed under my grip. I had scared her with my antics, but now that she knew the source of my distress, Sally seemed to breathe easier. "She's fine, Teddy. Absolutely fine. Timothy is looking after her."

I collapsed back onto the bed. Penelope was fine. Nothing else mattered to me for the moment, even me.

Sally wasn't quite so narrow-minded. While she liked Penelope, she loved me, so for her, the priorities were a little different. "You're going to be fine, Teddy," she assured both me and herself. "The doctors say the muscles around your throat were bruised, but your thorax was not seriously damaged. You simply need to rest for a couple of days, and then you'll be good as new."

Good as new, but for how long? I ran my fingers across the bruised and bloated skin around my throat and winced at the pain. I would try to limit what I would say, at least for now. Overall I was glad my voice was okay. In this era of talking pictures I needed my voice to make a living, but what about the rest of me? Someone had tried to kill me. Had nearly killed me. Why was I still alive?

Time to get some answers. "How did I get here?"

"When the hospital got the call, a couple of interns were dispatched and brought you in an ambulance."

"When they got the call? Who called them?" Who stopped the killer from squeezing the last bits of air from my lungs? What the hell was going on? I remembered the conversation I had overheard when I'd woken up. "Did I hear someone say something about a stalker?"

She pushed her lips together, tight. For a moment I was afraid I had offended her somehow, but then I realized she was trying not to laugh. "Very well, then." She headed toward the door. "I was going to have them wait until you were stronger, but since you insist."

Before her white gloved hand finished pulling the door open, a young girl flew into the room. She rushed to my bedside, talking a mile a minute. "Oh, Mr. Wainwright," she gushed, "I am simply your biggest fan. I read every article about you in the movie magazines, and have your pinup over my bed. I have been watching your movies simply forever, or at least since I was ten, which has been forever. Seven years seems like forever, watching you grow old on screen, anyway..."

I blinked as she went on, wondering if it was really possible for so many words to tumble out of one mouth without pausing for a breath. I waited for the girl to collapse from lack of oxygen, but it didn't happen. She just kept on talking. Sally stood behind the young dynamo, laughing. Beside her stood a young man, quietly twisting his hat. He gazed at the talking young girl next to me with a mixture of love and fear. The boyfriend, I assumed.

Something had to be done. I latched my fingers around her arm. The sudden contact startled her enough that, wonder of wonders, she actually stopped for a minute. Long enough for me to ask a question. "Name?"

She seemed startled by the inquiry. "You don't remember your name? Oh, dear. I thought the doctors said you were going to be fine, but now there's brain damage, and memory loss, and who knows what else."

I shot a desperate look toward Sally who finally took pity on me. "I believe he wants to know your name, dear."

"Oh." The girl's mouth blossomed into a great, big smile. "My name is Trudy Granger."

Right then I decided she was kind of sweet, when she wasn't talking. I let go of her arm, and reached for her hand to shake, like adults did.

Her eyes grew so round and her face so flushed as she stared at our clasped hands, I was afraid she might faint. Trudy squealed. "Oh, Billy. Did you see that?"

A quiet murmur came out of the sad sack next to Sally, and I figured that was all we were going to hear from him. The perfect boyfriend for Trudy. The girl had already lost interest in Billy and was staring at her hand like it was a rare and beautiful sculpture. "I am never, ever going to wash this hand again."

Well, I thought. That vow would become a problem at times, like say after mucking about in the garden. How would you get all the dirt off of your fingers if you couldn't wash them?

There my mind went, wandering off again. Trudy was gearing up for another soliloquy, so I spoke up, asking her what had happened.

The young girl blinked. She was concentrating more on my handsome face rather than my question. I shook her hand again, this time to get her attention. She blinked again, and finally returned to her natural, constantly talking state. "What happened? Oh, out on the road you mean?" When I nodded she carried on. "You see, I desperately wanted your autograph. Well, that isn't exactly true. I do have your autograph, on a picture. I sent away for it and it's sitting on my bedside table. Anyway, it wasn't enough. I wanted an autograph from you personally. So when winter vacation finally came I had Billy get his jalopy and we started following you."

I had been followed? By a crazy seventeen-year-old fan? I had no idea. I was going to have to sharpen my private detecting skills.

"After days of trying, we got nowhere. Say, where'd you disappear to anyway?"

Instant redemption. Apparently I wasn't as bad at detecting as I had feared. Trudy must have lost track of me while Jenkins was working at the Imperial Palms Hotel.

Trudy rolled right on. "So today I was determined to finally pin you down for my autograph. Billy and I followed you, but the road was so bumpy we lost track of you for a little while. Then we finally caught up and saw that a horrible man was trying to kill you."

Finally, we were getting somewhere. "Did you see what he looked like?"

"I'm sorry, but he was all covered up. I thought it odd, he

was all wrapped up in an overcoat, wearing a scarf around his face and his hat pulled down low. Here this guy was dressed for the dead of winter in New York, but we're here in sunny Southern California where it never really gets so cold, even in November. He was such an odd duck." Not odd at all, if you wanted to keep your identity a secret while you were killing someone. I waved toward Trudy and she continued with her story. "Anyway, I couldn't let this man kill you before I got my autograph."

Of course not. Would she have left me there to die if she already had my signature clutched in her hot little hands? Hopefully I would never have to find out.

"So anyway, I started shouting to get the man's attention, while Billy waved a tire iron he'd gotten out of the trunk. I guess we scared him enough so he dropped you and ran away." She actually stopped for a second, long enough to really look at me. "I'm sorry you got hurt."

What an amazing girl. Very strange, but amazing. I reached for the pad and pen resting on the nightstand, and scribbled a few lines. When I was done I ripped the page out and held it out toward her. "Thank you, my dear Trudy. Thank you so very much for saving my life."

Her eyes widened. Imagine, after all this, I actually managed to surprise her. She reached forward with a trembling hand to clasp her beloved prize, but when she got close enough I grabbed a hold of her again, pulling her down so I could kiss her cheek. Her squeak of delight was so loud I was nearly deafened.

"Oh, Billy. Did you see that?"

He had.

We all had.

I wondered if she would ever wash her face again, and decided I was better off not knowing.

∗

When the whirlwind named Trudy exited my room, and hopefully my life, with my autograph clutched safely in her hand, a relative peace fell upon me. Sally had to mock me about my new "girlfriend" but I let her have her fun. Revenge was, a dish best served cold. Finally she tired of tormenting me and shared some studio gossip instead.

Apparently the press had renewed its singular interest in me, but for an entirely different reason. Treating Montgomery's murder as if it were old news, now they were busy speculating on the attempt on my life. Some thought a former lover I had spurned had come back for revenge, which was ridiculous. Not to say I didn't have a former lover or two—I was a red-blooded American male after all—but I made it a rule to part on good terms with anyone I was ever in a relationship with. I had seen far too much animosity in my life. I refused to engage in ill will any further. When it came to information of real import, Sally had little to offer. In the hours since I had been brought to the hospital, she hadn't heard a peep from anyone official about my murder attempt, Montgomery's death, or Harrington. It was Harrington's current whereabouts that bothered me the most. Was he behind bars? Had he fled to Mexico? Not knowing was driving me crazy.

Nightfall came, and Sally went to retrieve my beloved Penelope from Timothy and take them both to her apartment for a good meal. While I enjoyed Sally's company, I was happy to have a moment or two to myself. But that's only how long it lasted, and then Sheppard walked into my room.

He didn't even get a chance to say anything before I pounced. "Did you find the gun?"

"Sorry Wainwright. By the time I got to Harrington's place, the gun was gone. He must have become suspicious and ditched it."

"Damn." Maybe he was going to get off scot-free after all. "What about me?"

"You think Harrington was the one who tried to strangle you on the road?" Sheppard was no dummy. He picked up on my concerns without my having to spell things out. "I'm not so sure he's our guy."

"How can you say that? I've been chasing after Harrington for days. He saw me in front of Montgomery's building right after the murder. He has to know I'm a threat to him." I was going to say more, but a coughing fit ripped through my throat.

"Whoa, there, relax." His hand steadied my shoulder, and then Sheppard poured me a glass of water. "I'm not saying he isn't our killer. It just seems like he's a little too self-absorbed to be running around the countryside strangling people, that's all."

"He would if he thought I was a threat to the thing he values most in the entire universe, himself."

"I suppose so." Sheppard patted my shoulder again. Two friendly gestures from the guy. I almost swooned. "Don't worry, I'm having a couple of the fellas keep an eye on him, just in case."

"Good. I don't think I'm being unkind when I say Harrington is no intellectual. Perhaps he'll make a mistake."

"Maybe he'll slip up when he tries for you again," the inspector said with a bit too much cheer for my taste.

"Thanks so much for your support."

Sheppard barked out a laugh, the first I'd heard from him, and then reached for his hat. "My boys will be keeping an eye on you too. They might try to save you in time." He flashed me a smirk, and was gone.

Apparently I was now classified as bait. I hope this new role wouldn't turn out to be my last one.

**

When morning came, I woke to find someone sitting in the chair next to my bed. He held a newspaper in front of his face, but I was pretty sure it was a man. Sally had much nicer legs than this person, and they were very rarely hidden by trousers. Tweed trousers, which were the same color and texture of the pants that Timothy often wore.

Part of his left wrist and hand protruded from the newspaper print. I caught a flash of gold and sat up straighter in the bed. Sunlight beamed through the window and reflected off a metal band encased around the wrist, making it shine. Timothy's wristwatch. I had seen the watch many times, but hadn't paid much attention to it before. Timothy had said his father had given it to him upon his graduation from college, but now it drew my interest. Looking closer I could see the band made up of separate gold colored links. I thought back to those black gloved fingers clamped around my neck, and recalled feeling little pieces of metal beneath my fingertips as I struggled. Pieces of metal that I couldn't identify before, but could very well links in the band of a wristwatch. I shivered. My attacker was wearing a gold wristwatch very similar to the one Timothy was wearing right now.

An unpleasant thought crossed my mind. Could it have been Timothy who attacked me on the road? No, I thought. It must've been Harrington. Harrington was the one with the motive. Timothy had no reason to kill me, but Harrington did.

I was trying to ignore that I'd seen no watch on Harrington's wrist in either of our encounters, nor had I found such a watch in his room. Perhaps one of his lady friends had just given it to him, a token of her esteem. Perhaps.

There had to be some other explanation. Timothy wasn't a killer. It wasn't in his nature, was it? But what did I really know about him? We didn't talk much outside of work. I knew he wasn't married, and he seemed not to have a girlfriend at the moment, but little else. We never really talked about growing up, or our families, but that was a subject I had little interest in exploring with anyone. I was happy not to have my family brought to my attention repeatedly and I'd just assumed it was the same with him.

I thought back to when Timothy caught me in Montgomery's office, wearing my cleaning lady outfit. Before he'd realized who I was, he'd walked in furious at Montgomery. More angry than I had ever seen him before. Was he angry enough to kill? I didn't know, and right now it bothered me, very much.

The paper dropped and Timothy gave me a smile which only offered warmth and friendship. I returned the smile, but it was a hollow one. It was wrong to suspect this man, yet I did, and would continue to do so until I uncovered the truth.

I don't know how I did it, but somehow I was able to engage in ordinary conversation with Timothy, for the entire hour he stayed. We talked about nothing consequential, but Timothy assured me he would enjoy taking care of Penelope whatever I wished. After a while a nurse shooed him out, saying I needed to rest. With a jaunty wave he left me alone, with my thoughts, which were busily engaged.

I would not be able to rest easy until I knew for sure about Timothy. I asked the nurse if I could use a telephone. She politely turned her back while I gathered my dressing gown around me, and then she escorted me to the phone resting on the nurses' desk. Thanking her profusely, I waited until she was out of earshot, and I called the nearest telegraph office to send a very special wire. It was addressed to my old commander in the army. Despite his current status as a trader of wheat futures in the stock market, I strongly suspected he still had his fingers in certain informational pies. If anyone could tell me about Timothy's background, he could.

CHAPTER SIX

I felt the heated kiss of a sunbeam against my face, the glass from the window barely lessening its intensity. I leaned back, my eyes falling shut, and enjoyed the warmth for a moment. Unfortunately that was all I had, a moment. My peace was disrupted by a rustling sound, and suddenly the warmth on my face was gone. I opened my eyes and saw a wall of fur, blocking my view of the window. Penelope had inserted her body between me and the sun, ensuring that all the heat from the beams fell upon her. With a satisfied purr, she turned around a couple of times, and settled down in a half circle with her head resting on her paws. She closed her eyes, and began what I suspected was a good long nap.

I wasted a moment being jealous, but if I wanted to, I could spend the day taking a good long nap too. I had tried that yesterday when I'd gotten out of the hospital, and returned to my luxury suite at the hotel in Beverly Hills, and it had bored me to tears.

In my defense, I did make valid attempts to rest, lying on the bed or sitting on the chaise lounge, reading the newspaper.

The sometimes-informative and sometimes-titillating content within the newsprint was able to hold my interest, at least for little while. After catching up on politics and baseball scores, I steeled my nerve and turned to the Hollywood gossip section. While it was not surprising to see that half the page was filled with some details and lots of innuendo about my near-death experience on the road, the other half was devoted to another scandal, one I knew nothing about. I read with interest, happy to be off the news hot seat for change. Then I discovered that this latest hubbub involved someone at RKM Studios.

Oh dear.

While I wasn't directly involved, thank God, I did know a couple of the people mentioned in the headlines, including my dear *friend*, Lance Hudson. Lance was the solo star of the *Perry Wallace* films, but even he couldn't act in a vacuum. One of the supporting cast members was a man named Trevor Caldwell, who played the standard dull-witted cop in the films, a character that Inspector Sheppard hated. I had only seen Caldwell a couple of times at a few parties, but I didn't really know him well at all. Now that I thought about it, I wondered if anyone knew much about him. He always seemed to stand just behind Lance Hudson, with his hat in his hand, never saying much. Never the center of attention.

No more. Caldwell was getting plenty of attention now. Apparently his automobile had gotten into a little accident at the corner of Sunset and Fountain in the wee hours of the morning. The damage to the car wasn't bad, just a fender bender really, and no one had been hurt, but it was Caldwell's career that was the true victim in the crash. Some enterprising reporter discovered that the companion in the car was not Caldwell's wife. At first, this tidbit did not impress me. So what if he had an affair? Even in these Farnsworth decency code days, going out on the town without your wife wasn't such a horrific thing. Then I read further and discovered that the young lady wasn't your usual sort of trollop. No, she was his wife's younger sister. Now there were calls which ranged from firing Caldwell immediately, to cutting his head off and putting it a top a pike.

Poor RKM Studios. If you counted Montgomery's death, my near-death on the road and now this, that was three major scandals hitting the studio in one week. Montgomery must have been spinning in his grave.

Once I finished with the papers, I was left with not much else to do. I listened to the radio for a while, ordered room service, and paced. The walls were getting to me. I had been confined too much recently, and now I desperately wanted out.

It was too late to attempt a trip back to the valley. I had no desire to risk being caught out on the road again, at least until this killer was caught. Besides, I was starting the next *Detective Tompkins* movie in a few days. Even if I made the arduous trek successfully, I would only have a few hours at the orchard before I had to come back.

Since I would be heading back to work soon anyway, perhaps the safest place for me right now was behind the tall walls of RKM Studios. Safe from the press, the public and any frenzy the world wanted to toss at me. When I rang Sally up to tell her my plan, she was against it at first, fearing I was going to do too much too fast. I had to repeatedly assure her that I was not going to do any hard work at least for today. Memorizing lines and rehearsing scenes I would save until tomorrow.

Keeping in mind the image of a certain young woman, I

decided to take care of a chore that I had been neglecting, answering my fan mail. I got plenty of letters each week from girls all over the country, each in love with my handsome face. Sometimes I borrowed a secretary from the pool to answer in my name, but I tried to do it myself whenever I had a chance. When I arrived at the lot, I went to my little bungalow, and grabbed a stack of letters, studio publicity pictures of me—no, I didn't keep any in a frame in my room—a couple of good stout pens, and settled myself in my writing desk, which was positioned right next to the window to get the aforementioned sun.

I spent an hour or so reading letter upon letter where young, and some not so young, women professed their love to me. Some even proposed marriage. A couple of the letters were scary, the women expressing their intense feelings in sometimes graphic terms, but most made me smile and some even made me laugh. I must've signed a picture like this for Trudy sometime in the past, never dreaming that it would eventually save my life. I petted my cat, and reached for a glass of iced tea resting beside me. It was nice not having to worry about murderers or anything of the like for a little while. All I had to do was sign my name on a photo, add a personal inscription, tape the girl's address to the back, and put it in a pile. In a while Davy from the mailroom would come by and pick them up. Even though he was only sixteen, Davy was bright and quick. I trusted that he would work hard to make sure all of these photos were packaged and properly mailed.

Maybe I would sign a photo for my new bodyguard. Despite his teasing that I would be bait, Sheppard hadn't left me in the lurch. Yesterday he called to tell me not to worry if I spotted a big fella in a dingy suit with a mashed up nose following me around. He was an intrepid law man. Yes, he was intrepid, so much so that he was snoozing under a tree outside my bungalow door.

I didn't know where Harrington was snoozing, or even if he was working. The cowboy film had wrapped up shooting while I was in the hospital. If Harrington hadn't suddenly gained some smarts and fled to Mexico, odds were he would come sniffing for work soon enough. His ego wouldn't allow him to stay off screen for long.

The logical place to go get information was the casting office, but I wanted to keep my contact with Timothy at a minimum until I got an answer to my wire. While I was an excellent actor, I wasn't sure I could keep my suspicions hidden from a friend of mine. So it was best to keep as far away from Timothy as I could, until I understood the situation a little better.

I picked up the phone and called Sally, and asked her to ask Timothy about Harrington for me. She wanted to know why I didn't talk to him myself, so I had to make up a story. I told her I was afraid Penelope preferred his company to mine, and I wanted to keep my distance for the time being, yet I didn't want to hurt Timothy's feelings. Sally knew full well that I was an insane idiot when it came to my cat, so she simply accepted the story for the crazy thing it was and agreed to call Timothy on my behalf.

While I waited I returned to my pictures and spent another hour reading about undying love and getting writer's cramp. Then the phone rang.

"Teddy," she sounded a bit breathless. "You better get to the administration building right away."

"Why? What's going on?"

"A few minutes ago I decided to take a break. I wanted to get out of the writers' bungalow a while, so I decided to go see

Timothy to ask about Harrington, rather than calling on the phone."

"And?"

"And he nearly crashed into me when he was storming out of his office."

"Timothy, storming?"

"Something is terribly wrong right now. He barely apologized to me before saying he had to go see Mr. Owens immediately. Then he went striding toward the administration building. I have never seen him so upset."

"Strange." I remembered the scene in Montgomery's office shortly before he was murdered. Timothy was upset about a change in casting then. Could something similar have set him off now?

"Teddy, I don't know what's going on, but I'm afraid something terrible might be happening," Sally said. "I think you should go to Mr. Owens office right now and find out what's going on."

"Yes," I said as I reached for my coat and hat. "I think you're right. I will call you as soon as I know something."

"Thank you Teddy."

Penelope was still snoozing in the sunlight. She would be fine on her own for a while, so I headed out the door to find out what the hell was going on.

***

I heard raised voices, even as far as the hallway, which surprised me. Montgomery's—I mean, Owens'—private office was soundproof, as I recalled. Even if the inner door was opened, I shouldn't have been able to hear so clearly. When I reached the outer office, I saw why. Mrs. Sylvia Rivers had been the executive secretary at RKM Studios for nearly a decade. Now in her mid-forties, she was always impeccably dressed, sometimes in blue, and sometimes in gingham, but regardless of the color, she was always in command of any situation. She would have made a perfect school teacher—stern, precise, and a stickler for the rules—until now. I stood in the doorway of the outer office, gripping the door handle, afraid my eyes were going to pop right out of my head like they did in some of those cartoons made by RKM Studios' competitors. For there was Mrs. Rivers, prim and proper Mrs. Rivers, hunched over her desk, with an ear to the office intercom. An intercom that was broadcasting an argument coming from the confines of Owens' inner office to the entire outer room.

Why that little minx. Who knew she had this in her?

I stepped forward. She was startled when she saw me, her hand reaching for the shutoff switch, a red flush filling her face. I placed a finger over my smiling lips to shush her, and winked to let her know everything was going to be okay. She moved her hand away from the switch, and settled back in her chair. I gestured toward her, a silent request to join her. She hesitated for just a moment, and then nodded. I moved before she could change her mind. I perched half my ass on the edge of her desk and leaned forward as we both listened.

"Owens, are you out of your mind?" The fury in Timothy's voice came across the speakers loud and clear.

"I do not understand what the difficulty is, Mr. Edmunds," Owens was a little bit harder to hear, which was not a surprise. He was essentially a mouse in human clothing. The only reason he had a job at RKM Studios at all was because he was the nephew of a silent movie queen who had once been a big presence on the lot. But now both the movie queen and Montgomery were gone, and I suspected Owens soon would be as well. "You know what happened to Trevor Caldwell this weekend. His part in the *Case Files of Percy Wallace* films must be recast immediately."

"Yes I understand that," Timothy replied. "And I have several good candidates in mind, but now I've come to find out that you have already cast the part, and you gave it to Chad Harrington."

What! My body jostled, and I nearly tumbled off Mrs. Rivers' desk and onto the floor. I couldn't have heard that right. They couldn't have really given Caldwell's role to Harrington?

"Yes," Owen said. "Chad Harrington now has that role."

My stomach was churning. Was I about to throw up?

"Good God man!" Timothy sounded almost a nauseous as I. "Harrington is no actor. He can't pretend to be somebody else. He's too busy flaunting himself."

"His skills or lack thereof aren't really your concern," Owens said.

"What?" Timothy sounded so worked up I was afraid he might give himself a stroke. "I am the head of casting at this studio. It's my name at the end of every film credit. If a movie goes down because of a poor casting choice, it is a reflection upon me, not to mention a financial disaster for everyone else here."

"None of that matters!" Both Mrs. Rivers and I reared back. We had never heard Owens raise his voice before. "The decision has been made. Harrington begins shooting on the *Case Files* set within the hour, and that is final."

Nothing came through the intercom except for heavy breathing, presumably while Timothy was trying to take this all in. I was working hard to deal with it myself. What the hell was Owens doing? Why risk a production that made money for the studio by putting such an unqualified doofus in an important role?

Then came shouts, so loud I could hear them clearly through the wooden door, as well as through the intercom. "The hell this is final! I'm putting in a call to the board in New York. We'll see what they have to say. This isn't over."

Owens may have made some reply, but I didn't have time to hear it. The inner office door burst open. I didn't want Timothy to see me so I ducked beneath Mrs. Rivers' legs—I mean to say I dived underneath Mrs. Rivers' desk. She gasped in surprise, and I patted her calf in reassurance, and hunkered down to make myself as small as possible.

It didn't matter much anyway. Timothy was so furious, he stormed with right out of the office. I waited until his rapid footfalls could no longer be heard, and then I stood up, straightened my tie, and held out my hand to Mrs. Rivers. "Thank you my lovely lady for an entirely delightful and entertaining afternoon. Know well that the bouquet of roses you will receive in the next twenty-four hours shall be from me." Then when she put her hand in mine, I raised it up to my lips and kissed it. Her giggle was reassuring. She was enchanted by my antics, and not furious enough to call a cop to throw me into jail for being a masher. I decided to get out of there before Owens came out as well, so I gave her a jaunty salute, and was out the door.

Standing on the front steps, I was pleased that I knew now where Harrington was going to be for the next few days. But the thought of him paired up with Lance Hudson was downright mind-boggling. Two titanic egos, on the same set at the same time. Who would be the victor? It was guaranteed to be a spectacle, and I wanted to be there to see every moment.

My bodyguard leaned gently against a nearby tree. I waved to him. "Come on, I think you and I are going to have a hell of an afternoon."

***

The red light was off when we arrived at Soundstage 16, meaning it was safe to enter. They were between takes. The giant stage doors that were used to allow large set walls and heavy film equipment access were tightly shut. We chose to enter through the smaller, human-sized door to the side.

On the way over, I learned more about the detective Sheppard had sent to keep an eye on me. He could be perfectly typecast as a detective, or a villain with the face he had, especially with his most striking feature: a nose, which was pretty much mashed flat. He gave the impression that he was an uneducated goon, but as I had learned long ago, looks could be deceiving. His name was Brooks and his nose had acquired its current mashed shape, not in some fight with a bootlegger making a run, but when he was playing baseball at Yale. An unfortunate altercation with the pitcher had resulted in the ball making contact with Brooks' nose at a very high velocity. Brooks had been on his way to acquiring a law degree when the war intervened. Ah, a fellow veteran. We exchanged war stories and the more we talked, the more confident I became. When I'd first seen Brooks I'd wondered if Sheppard had foisted the class idiot upon me, as payback for those idiot policemen on the screen. This caricature couldn't be farther from the truth. Perhaps Brooks would be able to save me after all.

Our conversation abruptly came to a halt when we stepped inside the soundstage. People ran back-and-forth and were talking up a storm, enjoying the freedom to speak that came with the camera being still. We cautiously stepped between the darting people who carried clipboards and scripts in their hands.

The actual set was positioned in far corner of the room, and was flanked by cameras and sound equipment. The space had been transformed into a typical waterfront bar, the type you find near the ocean in a bad part of town. There were the obligatory shoddy tables and chairs filling most of the room, with a giant bar stretching across the back of the set. The extras were dressed in nautical fair—striped shirts topping white dungarees. In the corner, a couple of musicians, also dressed in nautical clothes, warmed up the piano, and a tin whistle. They would provide background music to the scene, which would add an authentic feeling to the atmosphere.

There were no signs of the principals, of course. Lance wouldn't show his face outside of his dressing room until the director was ready for his presence on the set. No point in being with the riff-raff until you had to, but there wasn't any sign of Harrington either.

Strange.

The director, Adam Graham, was holding intense discussions with the camera man and script girl, while the rest of the set was filled with technical types. They all dashed back and forth, adjusting lights, and checking audio equipment. Only a few years ago, you could shoot five or six movies on the same stage at the same time. Then came the talking motion picture, which tripled the amount of equipment needed to record sound for posterity, and everything changed.

Filming took longer than it used to as well, which annoyed some people, but most of the extras didn't seem to mind. They held bottles, and some seemed to be partaking of a sip or two. I suspected if I looked closely I would find no cellophane tape wrapped around the neck of the bottles the men were enjoying.

There were two types of props on a set. The real deal and

the fakes made up to look like the real thing. When it came to bottles, standard prop tradition was to use the tape around the neck. It would never show up on camera, so it was an easy way sort out the phonies from the real thing.

A not-so-quiet curse found my ear. I followed it to its source, and saw the prop master staring with woe at a box of drinking bottles. "Trouble, Harry?"

"One of these sugar bottles has been left out too long."

Oh dear. We couldn't go around smashing real bottles over the skulls of our stuntmen or extras. They would all end up in the hospital, or perhaps the morgue. Since filmmaking was all about making the fake seem real, ergo the sugar bottle. Fake glass made by dissolving sugar in water and heating it to something called the "hard crack" stage, broke so convincingly it seemed like the real thing. An excellent choice for stunts. Unfortunately, if not set right, it didn't hold up well under the hot lights of a movie set. We were looking at one such example now. The bottle Harry held up was bulging around the middle, resembling more of a pregnant cow rather than a bottle of whiskey.

Brooks inspected it closely. "It looks like an exhibit I saw at the modern art museum."

"It sure as hell doesn't belong in a sea-front saloon." Harry reached out to toss it into the trash when I stepped in to intervene. "Hold on there." I took the misshapen bottle from him. "We'll take care of this for you."

"Much obliged."

He went back to putting the fake bottles on areas of the set where they would be used later.

I cracked our misshapen reject against the edge of a nearby table, where it satisfactorily broke into several big chunks, and handed a piece of the sugar glass to Brooks to enjoy. No sense in letting good candy go to waste.

As we enjoyed our treat, the noise level dropped around us. The director had finished his little huddle and he was ready for the next take. I hustled Brooks over to the side where we would be out of the way, yet still have a good view of the proceedings.

The assistant director called for the principals. After a brief interval came the arrival of the great Lance Hudson. He couldn't just walk through the door like everybody else: he had to pause at the edge of the set and wait for everyone to notice him. Everyone did. The cast and the crew stared at him with awe, or was it fear, as the great one made his way across the room to take his place in front of the cameras. No one spoke with him, no one touched him. Hell, most barely looked at him as they made last minute adjustments to the camera and the lighting. Despite the need for quiet in this age of sound recording, there was usually a little chitchat behind the scenes until the camera started to roll, but not here. This was the quietest set I had ever been on in my life. Perhaps my dislike of Lance was justified.

Brooks nudged my arm and drew my attention to the human-sized door we had used earlier. Harrington had just arrived. Brooks stood up a little straighter, his hand hovering near his pocket. I wondered if there was a gun in there. Harrington glanced around the set, passing his gaze over us without a pause, before focusing in on Lance. Strange. He saw me and had no reaction. It was as if I didn't matter to him in the least. As I watched him confidentially cross the room, a tiny bit of doubt crept in. What if he wasn't our killer after all?

"Here I am," Harrington's voice shattered the silence, fracturing the awkward peace that had settled upon the stage. He ignored the horrified glances from the crew, and strode right up to Lance, grabbing his hand and shaking with all his might.

"It is such a pleasure to be joining your cast, Mr. Hudson. I am sure my ample talents will bring greatness to your little production here."

Tense gasps and hunched shoulders circulated throughout the crew. No one had ever been so bold as to greet Lance in such a manner here.

To give him credit, Lance didn't shout or scream, he merely tilted up his chin so he could look down his nose at the insignificant creature that had dared to address him. Slowly, carefully, and very precisely, Lance extracted his hand from Harrington's grip. Lance turned his back on Harrington, and looked toward the director's chair. With every step Lance took toward the director, the director seemed to slouch further into his canvas seat. "Mr. Graham, who is this person?"

I felt so sorry for Graham. He was one lone director, surrounded on all sides by titanic egos, and no way out. "He's the man Mr. Owens has chosen to replace Mr. Caldwell."

"I see."

I didn't envy Owens either, but he brought this on himself. I suspected he would be getting a very heated telephone call as soon as this scene wrapped. For a change I found myself actually cheering for Lance to succeed.

Harrington, of course, was totally oblivious to the underlying consequences of his actions. "Yes sir, Mr. Hudson, I will be a real asset to your picture. I don't know why no one has ever utilized my talents before, but after the fans see me next to you in this movie we are going to fly right up to the top."

"We shall see." Three little words, each spoken with a precise and lengthy pause between them. It made me wonder what Lance was capable of when he was really and truly pressed. Lance made no further comment. He simply pulled out his pocket watch to check the time. "We are falling behind schedule. We shall go ahead for now." He shot a glance toward Graham. "We will deal with casting issues later."

The director gulped, and then the sound was buried as the crew scurried into place. An assistant directed Harrington toward his mark, which he promptly ignored, instinctively heading toward the best spot in front of the camera instead. The place where Lance was supposed to be. When Harrington got in range, Lance put the tip of his finger against Harrington's chest and pushed. Such a simple gesture, yet it seemed to penetrate through the self-absorbed haze that floated inside Harrington's mind. Harrington said nothing further, but went quietly to his correct spot, and finally shooting began.

In this scene, Lance's character was meeting with a cop, played by Harrington, in this waterfront bar. They were supposed to speak for several minutes before an argument next to them would break out and a typical bar fight would begin. They filmed several takes successfully. The only incidents were Harrington striving to get the best camera angle without actually moving his feet. It was so pathetic really. The man was simply a terrible actor. A part of me was happy. This would only make Detective Tompkins look better in comparison, but I couldn't suppress my growing horror as the debacle wore on. No one should be enforced to endure this, not even Lance.

Finally, they reached the big fight scene. A stunt double took Lance's place, and Harrington took his own place at the bar.

"Hey," Brooks said. "Shouldn't they use a stunt man for Harrington too?"

"Very observant, Detective," I said, "and quite correct. Normally stunt men replaced the principal actors in dangerous scenes, but Harrington would never let anyone take his place in front of the camera, even for a moment. His ego wouldn't allow it.

Since Lance's work was done for the moment, he headed toward the exit, and for his trailer, but not before stopping to have a private word with his stuntman. The conversation only lasted a moment or two, and then he was gone.

The cast and crew did a quick rehearsal. They specifically practiced the part where Harrington's character, this time played by Harrington himself, was going to be hit over the head with a whiskey bottle. Then Graham ordered everyone to their proper place and the film began to roll. For the next several minutes there was the usual amount of furniture breaking and fists swinging, all pulled back just a fraction before knuckles made actual contact against skin. I knew from experience that if you're hit hard enough with sugar glass, it was going to hurt. Not seriously injure you, but it would cause some pain.

I spotted Lance leaning against the side wall with his arms crossed, watching intently. Hmm. Lance never came out of his dressing room if he wasn't being filmed, so why was he standing there now? I scanned the room, looking everywhere, even off the set. Everything seemed to be proceeding along as normal. Chairs were breaking, and shouts were shouting as the scene built to its crescendo, but my unease was building as well. In fact, it was screaming at me.

Something was going to happen. Something out of the norm. Something terrible.

I had felt this way before, on the battlefields of France, just before cannon fire flew through our trench, ripping poor Smythson to bits. In the scene before me, a big burly extra grabbed one of the fake sugar bottles, and raised it, ready to smash it down upon Harrington's head.

Then I saw it.

"Stop!"

My shout was like a pitcher of cold water, shocking everyone and freezing them in place. For a moment all was still, but then Lance moved. A big cat defending his territory. "Wainwright," he hissed. "What the hell do you think you're doing?"

I ignored him, ran onto the set and grabbed the whisky bottle out of the stunt double's hand.

"Don't touch our props," Lance ordered, intercepting me. "I don't know what you think you are doing, Wainwright, but this is my set and my film, and I won't let your petty jealousy disturb things any further."

"Oh, shut up Lance," I had no patience for his delusions. "I'm trying to save a life here."

"What are you blathering about?"

"This." I held up the bottle. I gave him a moment to get a good look, but I could see he was still missing the point. I handed it over to the prop master instead. "Harry, please inspect this bottle, will you?"

"I don't see what for," Harry grumbled as he reluctantly came forward. "There's nothing wrong with—" He trailed off as he peered closer. "Oh, my dear."

"What is it?" Brooks had joined the party, his hand inside his pocket now. I knew then he was gripping a hidden pistol.

I gestured toward the bottle clutched in Harry's sweaty hand. "That bottle is real."

"What?" Lance drew forward, wanting a better look himself. "That's impossible."

"Look at it." We all did, but no one seemed to see what Harry and I saw. I pointed toward the neck. "Look at the neck."

Lance looked. "I don't see anything."

I nodded. "Exactly."

"This isn't the bottle I put out for the scene." Harry held it up. "See, there's no tape."

"No tape?" Hand still in his pocket, Brooks was still trying to understand why I was so suddenly afraid. "What kind of tape?"

"Prop masters put a piece of cellophane tape around the neck of bottles made out of sugar glass to sort them apart from the real thing."

Brooks began to catch on. "So that's a real bottle? Not one of those candy ones we munched on earlier?"

"Exactly," I said. "Someone switched the bottle after Harry put it on the bar. It probably happened when everyone was distracted by Harrington's grand entrance."

"Hey." Quiet until now, Harrington spoke up. "What's going on? Who cares about a little bottle? Why did you stop filming just before my big moment?"

I simply could not believe that any human being could be this self-absorbed, this oblivious to the world around him and survive into adulthood, but somehow Harrington had. "You should care." I forced the words out, now sorry I went to all the bother I'd gone through to save him. "Since someone just tried to kill you."

"What?" It seemed I had finally gotten his attention. Harrington gestured to the bottle, still clenched in Harry's sweating hands. "With that?"

"Yes. If this bottle hit you on the head full force, you could have easily been killed, or severely injured."

"Why in the world would anyone want to kill me?" Harrington asked.

Good question, dammit. Harrington was supposed to be the murderer, not the victim, and this little event was playing havoc with my theories. "I saw you outside Montgomery's office, dressed in that ridiculous disguise. You know I did."

"Did you like it?" The ass even had the gall to smile. "I thought I looked rather dashing in it, myself."

Did he just confess? "I ran into you minutes after Montgomery had been shot. No one else was there. You had to be the one to pull the trigger."

"Of course I pulled the trigger."

I was shocked frozen, not expecting a confession so easily. Brooks didn't freeze, however. The gun was out of his pocket and pointing Harrington's way.

"You admit that you killed Montgomery?" I asked.

"What? Now you're the one making no sense."

"How so?"

"Well, of course I did shoot Mr. Montgomery, as part of the plan, but I didn't kill him. He's still very much alive."

He sounded as if he really thought that Montgomery was alive. Either Harrington really was the best actor I had ever seen, or he really believed it.

Harrington noticed the gun in Brooks' hand, and finally some of that smug, self-confidence began to waver. "He is alive, isn't he?"

CHAPTER SEVEN

"Let me get this straight." Inspector Sheppard rubbed his temples, but it didn't seem to do much to relieve the tension I was sure was building inside his head. "You admit you shot Montgomery, but you also think he's still alive?"

If Harrington nodded any harder I was afraid he was going to dislocate his neck.

The inspector shot me a look. When we'd met I was the image of everything Sheppard hated, yet now I was the only lifeline he had left in a world otherwise gone mad. I wished I could reassure him, but all I could do was shrug. I was no longer surprised by anything that came out of Harrington's mouth. Amazed and appalled, sure, but not surprised.

After the near miss on the *Case Files* set, further shooting was canceled. Brooks had promptly sealed off the sound stage so no one could leave, and then had called for help. Shortly thereafter, a barrage of boys in blue had arrived, led by the intrepid Inspector Sheppard himself.

A team had immediately surrounded poor Harry, who had led them to a little alcove in the back where some of the props were kept. He had, no doubt, given them a lesson on how dangerous props were handled on a movie set. Things like ammunition, live rounds, blanks, and explosives were kept locked up in a special facility two buildings away. Other props, average things like books, false telephones, the obligatory detective's magnifying glass, and yes, whiskey bottles, were all in the alcove. Stages were never locked so anybody who had access to the sound-stage had access to the alcove. This fact narrowed down the suspects to pretty much anyone who worked at RKM. No help there.

I don't know if Sheppard had some sort of death wish, or if he was the type of fellow who wouldn't subject someone under his command to a dirty job he wasn't willing to undertake himself. In any case, Sheppard saved Harrington, Lance, and me for himself. The best for last I suppose. At least he appropriated the largest and nicest room next to the stage for our questioning. This, of course, was Lance's dressing room. A choice I wholeheartedly approved of. I would cherish the memory of Lance's face turning into a pickle when he realized he couldn't say no. Even the great Lance Hudson couldn't resist in the face of an LAPD badge.

I smiled right until I got through the door. Lance's dressing room was at least as twice as big as mine, with furnishings and decorations that had to come from the nicest Beverly Hills department store. While normally I wasn't the type of person to be jealous about such a thing, my Detective Tompkins was more popular than Lance's Perry Wallace, so it did hurt a little bit. I would have to take this up with Owens when this was all over.

For now I kept my opinions to myself, settling my rear end in Lance's easy chair. Lance's hawk-like gaze didn't miss this gesture. The actor clenched his fists and advanced toward me.

Who knew what mayhem he intended, but Sheppard cleared his throat, reminding us all that the long arm of the law was present. Lance halted, but he kept those piercing eyes right on me, while he sat on his luxurious couch. He crossed his arms and eye Sheppard. A mannequin wouldn't have been more stiff.

Harrington, upon seeing all the good seats already taken, decided that he would share the couch with Lance. He took only two steps when a beefy hand grabbed his collar and pulled him back. Sheppard could yank when he wanted to, and he not-so-gently deposited Harrington into a wooden chair. It was time to start the third degree.

"Not so fast," Sheppard said.

"But I'm a star of this picture," Harrington protested. "I deserve some proper treatment."

We all wanted to give Harrington the treatment, and in Lance's case, perhaps the treatment would involve knuckles against bare skin. "You are not the star this picture," Lance said, "and when we are done here I'll make sure your face will never appear on a frame of celluloid again."

"Enough," Sheppard called out. "Chairs, movies, and egos will all have to wait. I have a murder to solve." Sheppard pulled out a straight chair for himself and sat only inches away from Harrington. "Okay, let's go through this slowly. You admit that you shot R.K. Montgomery?"

"Oh, yes," Harrington certainly wasn't shy about it. "And I did a spectacular job of it too."

"Tell me about it."

"Well, I went to wardrobe that night and took the Masked Avenger costume."

Time for me to shoe in. "Why did you pick that particular costume?"

"He said it was a poetic choice and I agreed. After all, I

should have been cast as the Avenger, instead of ridiculous Trevor Caldwell. I mean look at the man, sleeping with his sister-in-law. Yet he was chosen for the part over me. Is there no justice in the world?"

Yes there was justice, I thought. Caldwell had talent, Harrington did not, but there was no room for reality and Harrington's world view.

"Wait a minute," I said. "Someone else chose the Avenger costume for you?"

"Of course. I said so, didn't I? You are an idiot."

I let the insult slide by. "Who chose it for you?"

"The man who gave me the gun, of course."

"What?" Sheppard barked. "Somebody gave you that gun?"

"Yes."

"Who?"

"The studio's new casting director."

"New casting director?" Timothy hadn't mentioned anything about a new casting director. Despite my suspicions about my friend, if Timothy had been replaced, I would've heard about it. Something was very wrong here. "This casting director, what is his name?"

"Oh, I'm so bad with other people's names, let me think." It took Harrington plenty of time to come up with it. A minute at least. "Ross, I think his name was. Taylor Ross."

"Ross?" I shook my head. "Never heard of him."

Was it a hint of pity I saw from Harrington? "Perhaps the studio heads didn't inform you of the change?"

He was insinuating that perhaps the studio wouldn't be casting me in the future, ergo I wouldn't need to meet the new casting director, which was simply ridiculous. Most casting directors I knew didn't go around handing out loaded weapons. "Tell us about the gun."

"Well, Mr. Ross introduced himself to me at a party a couple of weeks ago, and gave me his card. He said he was the new casting director for the lot. He said he had been watching me for quite some time now, and simply could not understand why I wasn't being offered more roles. A sentiment I hardly agree with."

Sheppard cut him off quickly, not willing to listen to another one of Harrington's tirades. "What happened next?"

"He said he had a couple of ideas that he thought could help my career, but he didn't want to talk about them at the party. Too many other people around. It wouldn't do to have them listen in on our plans."

"Oh, sure," I said.

"Go on," Sheppard ordered, losing his patience.

"Mr. Ross told me to call him when I had a free moment, which I did. He arranged to have us meet in a little coffee shop, and then he gave me a little screenplay. He said it was a blueprint of our new plan."

So this mysterious Mr. Ross gave Harrington a script, did he? I wonder if it was one of the ones I thumbed through when I was inside Harrington's room. Had I actually read about the plan to kill Montgomery and hadn't realized it?

Sheppard wasn't waiting for any answers. "So together you planned to kill R.K. Montgomery."

"No," Harrington seemed to glimpse the real world and understand. He was in real trouble here. Suddenly he was cooperating. "Mr. Ross had an idea that would not only give me an opportunity to show off my considerable acting skills to Mr. Montgomery, but help the studio too."

"How in the world," Lance sneered, "could you possibly be of assistance to this studio?"

"Well, Mr. Ross said I would be a great help with a new

publicity campaign. One that was to introduce a new celluloid detective to the world."

A new detective at RKM? I glanced at Lance and saw that this was news to him as well. Was there really room for another on-screen investigator at the studio? Not likely. "Ross said this was part of some publicity stunt?"

"Yes," Harrington nodded. "He told me there would be a camera rolling behind the wall, but I wasn't to look for it. That would be too obvious. I was simply to go into Mr. Montgomery's office as the Masked Avenger, read some carefully written lines, and then pretend to shoot him. Then I was to immediately leave and wait for further developments, so that's what I did."

"No, wait," I said, not understanding this at all. "How would shooting Mr. Montgomery be a publicity stunt?'

"Well," Harrington said, looking like he was thinking hard, perhaps for the first time in his life. "Mr. Ross said that Mr. Montgomery would need a lot of press if he was successfully to launch a new hero for RKM Studios. So he set up this stunt where I, dressed as the Masked Avenger, would pretend to kill him. After the story was in the paper for several days then Mr. Ross said he would give me new scenes, and I would come forth and solve the case. After that, Mr. Montgomery would reveal that he was indeed alive, and a new film series would be born."

Silence filled the room. It sort of made sense—at least I could see how Harrington would accept such a wild story as truth.

"Now, I want to make sure I understand this correctly," Sheppard said. "You thought shooting Montgomery was all part of an act?"

"Of course," Harrington seemed surprised by the question. "And I must say he was quite convincing as the victim. Making all the right noises, and slumping over the desk with a long, shuddering sigh. It was as if he was really dying."

Wow.

Okay, Harrington was officially the most conceded and self-centered person I had ever met. He had actually murdered a man and didn't know it.

"So, Harrington," I said. "You really think Montgomery is alive?"

"Of course he is," the extra insisted. "And my audition must have been successful, since I got the part in the *Case Files* movie."

Yes, the murder did lead to him getting that part. With Montgomery gone, Owens was in charge. He was the one who made that casting choice, but why? Did Owens have some connection to this mysterious Mr. Ross?

Sheppard wasn't thinking so far ahead. I had admired the policeman's vast reservoir of patience when it came to dealing with Harrington throughout this interview, but that patience had finally come to an end. "Are you crazy?" He lunged forward, grasped Harrington by the lapels, and hauled him upright. "Listen to me, R.K. Montgomery is dead! Really, truly dead, and you know who killed him?" Sheppard shook the extra. "You did! There were real bullets in that gun. You shot him, and you killed him!"

Any color that Harrington had in his face drained away, leaving him with a pasty white complexion. Sheppard's words had gotten through. "Mr. Montgomery can't really be dead. It was all part of an act, I tell you. That gun wasn't supposed to be real."

"But it was," Sheppard countered, "and when you pulled the trigger, you ended Montgomery's life."

"Oh, Lord." The enormity of what he had done finally reached him. The extra sank back into his chair and held his head in his hands. "It was just a prop, I tell you, just a toy," he muttered. It wasn't supposed to be real."

"It wasn't real to you," I said, "but Mr. Ross knew darn well that gun was loaded with real bullets."

Harrington may have pulled the trigger, but the man who handed him the gun was the real murderer. Harrington was just a weapon.

Sheppard asked a few more questions, but by then he had had enough of Harrington. He called Brooks in and had the extra taken away under "protective custody," meaning Harrington would not be heading to jail. Instead, he would spend the next few days in a room, one perhaps as nice as his room in the Imperial Palms. This would keep him safe until everything was resolved, and also Harrington would be on hand if Sheppard wanted him again.

Once Harrington had been removed from the room, Lance got to his feet and stared at me. He didn't speak, but I understood I was receiving an order just the same. I wouldn't fight this one. I got quietly to my own feet, and allowed Lance to enjoy his favorite chair. The actor sat down and ignored me, paying attention only to Sheppard. "Well then, Inspector, I assume now you are done with my room."

"You assume incorrectly. I have a couple of questions for you too."

"What?" It seemed that Harrington didn't have the corner when it came to conceit. Judging by his popping eyes, and his tense torso, it had probably never occurred to Lance until that moment that he could be a suspect too. "You can't dare to insinuate that I had anything to do with this fiasco."

"Insinuate I can, and insinuate I will."

Lance left the safety of his easy chair, lunging toward Sheppard with a finger outstretched. "Now see here, you little worm," He actually wiggled the finger in Sheppard's face. "I deal with snide little detectives like you every day. You can't talk to me this way."

First Harrington, and now this. Sheppard reached for his pocket, which could contain only one of two things: either handcuffs, or a gun. Neither one would bode well for Lance.

I grabbed the actor's arm and whispered, "This man has a real badge, a real gun and he doesn't care who you are. If you don't start making nice right now, you will be spending the night in jail, and this time it will be your picture on the front pages of the papers, a picture showing you behind bars. Do you want that?"

Lance didn't like it. He was used to being the one on top, the one fawned at by everyone he came into contact with, but unlike Harrington, Lance was intelligent. He saw where Sheppard's hand was, and decided to take the prudent course. "My apologies, Inspector. My emotions are running high at this time. How may I assist you?"

Sheppard made no move to remove his hand from his pocket, at least not yet. "Sit down."

Lance nodded briefly, then tugged down the ends of his waistcoat, straightened his tie, which had come askew in the hubbub, and sat down. He crossed his legs and leaned back. A man without a care in the world. I ended up on the couch.

Sheppard's hand left the vicinity of his pocket and he resumed his seat. "So, Mr. Hudson, someone told me that you spoke to your stuntman just before shooting began. Then you stayed on the set to watch, contrary to your normal routine. Care to explain?"

Lance looked over to me, wondering if I was the little

birdie that chirped, and I was. I had managed to whisper in Sheppard's ear shortly after he arrived. Now I appreciated the inspector's efforts to keep my name out of it. It would add only more trouble, trouble that had nothing to do with the attempt on Harrington. Fortunately, Lance was now a beacon of cooperation. "In light of the events that followed, I suppose I can see why my actions seemed a little bit sinister, but I can assure you, Inspector, murder was not in my plans."

"What were your plans?"

"To get that ridiculous little man off of my movie. I had no idea what Owens was thinking when he sent him to my set, but I wanted to make sure he would leave as soon as possible."

"And how was your stuntman going to help with that? By hitting him over the head with a real bottle?"

"No!" I had seen Lance performing for several years, and I believed that he wasn't acting now. He seemed to be a man telling the truth. "I told my stuntman to try to trip him up a little," Lance confessed. "To make him look like a buffoon in front of the camera. Then I was going to take the film later to Owens and use it to get Harrington kicked off of my movie. Everything was set, but before my stuntman could have the chance to interfere, Wainwright here stopped everything in its tracks."

By saving Harrington's life, I thought.

Sheppard had the stone face of an intrepid law man. "I'll accept what you said, Mr. Hudson, for now."

"Thank you Inspector." Lance got up, crossed the room, and opened the door. "Now I would appreciate it if you both got the hell out of here."

"Of course Lance," I said, smiling. Sheppard straightened just as eagerly as me. I think we'd both had enough titanic egos for one afternoon.

***

Once we were outside, Sheppard and I walked in compatible silence for a while. There was no sign of Brooks. Apparently Sheppard had taken over the duties of guarding my precious body for now.

My mind was whirling with all the latest developments in the case. I thought I'd had a clear picture of the situation, but the attack on Harrington had scrambled my assumptions and had left me with mashed up mess.

"I owe you an apology, Wainwright."

"You do?" My feet almost stumbled as my reputed half-step had apparently returned. "Apology for what?"

"For my behavior earlier." Sheppard stopped walking and faced me. "This whole time, you have been nothing but friendly and trying to help. Despite the fact that you are a big movie star, you treated me and my men as equals. Unlike that Hudson guy."

"Ah, you expected all movie stars to behave like Lance, is that it?"

"Yes I guess I did." Sheppard held out his hand. "I am sorry."

"No worries," I said as I shook his hand eagerly. "The world of filmmaking is the world of stereotypes, and I guess that even includes leading men."

"I guess it does." We continued walking. "Speaking of leading men, what did you think about Hudson's explanation?"

"I suppose I believe him, mainly because I can't think of any reason why he would want to kill Montgomery. Sure, he's not thrilled with my presence on the lot. I'm competition to him, but if he were going to resort to murder, I would think he would like to kill me and leave Montgomery alone. Even if he did somehow believe killing Montgomery would help his situation here, he certainly wouldn't let Harrington anywhere near his *Case Files* set."

"I agree with you on that. So we are back to square one."

"It appears so."

Two steps forward, one step back. Wasn't that how the old saying went? I had a new one. *Two steps forward, then you step into quicksand and your ankles are dragged down into a quagmire of a mess, and no matter how hard you struggle, you will never break free.* This was what the hunt for Montgomery's killer felt like.

"Well," I said, trying to cheer us both up. "At least we have a new lead, thanks to the appearance of this mysterious Mr. Ross." Of course, three hours ago, I was sure Harrington was a solid lead. Look how that one turned out.

"Yes." If Sheppard had been a seventeen year-old-girl, I would've said that was a giggle coming out of his lips. It was interesting how despair could manifest in different ways in different people. "Of course, we have no idea who Ross is or where he is."

"Minuscule details." Minuscule indeed. I now had to accept the simple truth. Harrington was not the criminal mastermind I originally made him out to be. He was just too big an idiot to fill the role. "So what's next?"

"Next, I send an artist over to Harrington, to see if the idiot can describe what this Ross looks like. Then, with a sketch, maybe we will have something to go on."

"Something," I agreed. "I suppose Harrington gave the gun back to Ross after the shooting."

"Either that or Ross told him to get rid of it, along with the Masked Avenger costume. We never did find it."

"That's right. I had forgotten about that."

"I think I'll accompany our sketch artist and clear up those little details with Harrington."

"If you can pry him away from the nearest mirror long enough to talk to him."

Sheppard shook his head. "I have been a police officer in this town for twenty-five years. I have investigated crimes ranging from mass murder to searching for a pet snake escaped from its owner. I thought I had seen it all."

"You mean you have never run across a man who killed someone and not even realized it?" I wasn't being sarcastic. If a character like Harrington ended up in a movie script, we would be laughed out of theaters nationwide. It was such an absurd situation.

"I have not, at least until today. I'm not sure my captain is going to believe me when I write up this report."

"Just make sure you don't take a little snort before handing it in. He may think you're having drunken hallucinations."

Sheppard barked a laugh. "I guess I'll need you as a character witness then."

"Any time."

"Inspector." Brooks joined us, slightly breathless from running from the parking lot. "We have Harrington squared away."

"Good. I'll be stopping by to see him soon." Sheppard began to fill Brooks in on what we had learned, or rather, what we hadn't learned from Lance.

A voice called my name. Young Davy ran toward me with an envelope clutched tightly in his hand. "Hi, Mr. Wainwright."

"Hey there, Davy." I waved toward the envelope. "What do you have there?"

"This just came into the mailroom marked urgent, so I thought I'd better bring it to you right away."

"Thank you Davy," I said digging in my pocket for a dollar. "That was quick thinking."

I flipped the coin toward him, and his eyes lit up when he snatched it from mid-air and saw how much it was. A dime would usually be a sufficient tip, but Davy's dad was out of work, and his family needed the money. I certainly could afford it. "Thank you very much sir."

"My pleasure, Davy. You run along now."

"Yes sir." He actually fired off a salute my way before he scampered back to the mailroom. How nice it was to be young, when everything in life was an adventure.

I held a standard business-sized envelope in my hand. As Davy said, it was marked urgent, but there was no return address in the corner. Strange. I peered closely at the postmark and saw it was from Hollywood, but other than that there was no indication as to who sent it. I felt the envelope, and found that it was fairly flat. No way to hide a gun in there. Still, I felt uneasy, so I opened it with care. I slid my finger under the gum flap, and carefully separated it from the rest of the envelope. I pulled the two sides apart, and saw that there was one folded piece of paper inside. Sheppard was still in deep conversation with Brooks. Neither man was paying any attention to me at the moment, which suited me just fine. Using two fingers only, I gently extracted the page out of the envelope, and placed the envelope on the ground near me. I carefully unfurled the paper.

My caution was justified. This was no love note from a star-struck young girl. There were only two sentences on the paper, and the words were made out of letters that were cut out one by one from a magazine. They were glued into place, spelling out a message. The paper shoot a little as I read it over carefully.

Keep your nose out of the Montgomery case, Wainwright. That is, if you want to keep on living.

I had been snooping around for several days, and only now I get a threat? Who could've sent it? It obviously wasn't from Harrington. This would be the kind of thing Lance would do, but he wouldn't be so subtle. I recalled my telegram to my old boss, inquiring about my dear friend Timothy. I hadn't heard back from him yet, which wasn't a surprise, as I only sent my query yesterday, but a telegram was not a secure form of communication. Anyone could've overheard my query at the nurses' station at the hospital, or perhaps someone was in the telegraph office itself was listening.

I should tell Sheppard about this threat. It had a direct connection to this case, yet I hesitated. Deep down I felt this had something to do with Timothy, and anything having to do with Timothy I wanted to keep to myself. Still, I wondered if sending the letter to a police laboratory would be helpful. An intrepid investigator could look over the paper with a magnifying glass and see if there were any fingerprints. But whoever sent this probably was a professional. He would not be so careless to carefully construct such a threat without wearing gloves. No, Sheppard would not see this, not yet.

I carefully returned the paper to the envelope, folded it, and put it in my pocket. I would keep this to myself for now, at least until I talked to Timothy.

Sheppard and Brooks had finished their conversation. Sheppard told me that Brooks would resume his post as my bodyguard while Sheppard went off to talk to Harrington. That was fine with me. I had a little chat of my own I wanted to engage in, and I didn't want a police inspector along when I had it.

***

Brooks kindly waited outside the casting office. I made my way through toward the back, not really caring if I stepped on a picture or two. Timothy was at his desk, hard at work. When he saw me, he smiled. "Ah Teddy, there you are. I heard about what happened on the *Case Files* set. It's unbelievable."

"It certainly is," I said as I sat down next to him. "Who would want to kill Harrington?"

"Well you know the answer to that, Teddy." I leaned forward slightly. Was Timothy going to confess right here and now? "Everyone who has ever met him wants to kill him."

I laughed at my friend's joke. A joke that was certainly true, but it was not helping me get any closer to finding out if Timothy was involved. "Still," I said, trying to draw him out. "It was strange that Harrington even got that part in the first place. I'm sure you didn't give it to him."

"I certainly did not." Timothy's voice was firm. "That order came straight from the top. In fact, I even went to Owens office to have it out with him, but I couldn't make him budge."

"You did?"

"I sure as hell did. It was my reputation on the line, my reputation that was going to be ruined along with the movie when Harrington got on screen, and it would cost the studio a heckuva lot of money. I do not understand why Owens signed off on such a bad choice."

"Neither do I."

Hmm. I certainly didn't have to work hard to get Timothy to tell me about the scene with Owens. It was hardly the actions of a guilty man. If anyone's actions were at question here, they were mine. Here I was, willing to believe that my friend could engage in something as nefarious as murder on the filmiest of evidence. So what if he had a wrist-watch similar to my strangler? That certainly wasn't enough to convict a man. Still, there was that death threat burning a hole in my pocket. It could have come from Timothy, or it could've come from the mysterious Mr. Ross.

A distressing thought occurred to me. What if Timothy and Mr. Ross were one and the same? My friend's warm smile was no longer enough to quell all my doubts, at least not yet. I would make no further progress confronting Timothy directly right now, so I said my goodbyes.

I was deep in thought as I headed back to my bungalow, with the ever-faithful Brooks walking two paces behind me. I needed more information, and I needed it now. I could no longer indulge in the luxury of waiting for a reply to my telegram. It was time to spend the money on a long distance telephone call.

***

I was certainly a lucky fellow today. I got ahold of a long distance operator right away and she said they actually had a line open. I wouldn't have to wait an hour or so to place my call. Profusely thankful for the miracle of modern technology, I settled back in my chair and petted Penelope while the phone rang.

It buzzed for a minute, then two, before the receiver was lifted and a lilting, female voice came across the wire. "Mr. Wiggins' office. Miss Thurgood speaking."

"Hello beautiful. How would you like an autographed photo from one of the most astounding and fascinating of all Hollywood stars?"

"Oh, Mr. Gable, is that you?" Her full-bodied voice didn't disguise her giggle.

"Very funny, Claire." I had met Claire Thurgood shortly after returning from France, while I worked for our clandestine employer in the weeks after the war. She was his executive secretary. In fact, she was the one who suggested I get into acting, so in a way, I owed her everything. A tally I was going to add to right now. "Listen my sweet, I sent the old man telegraph yesterday and I haven't heard back yet. Do you know if you got it?"

There was silence on the line, a long silence. So long I suspected something was up. I was about to say something when she finally spoke. "I'm not sure, Theodore. He did receive some sort of communiqué, but he said nothing to me about it. He simply grabbed his hat and headed off to his gentleman's club."

"Really?" That was quite enlightening. The club she was referring to was the place in Washington D.C. for men in Mr. Wiggins' line work to get together and talk shop, and I didn't mean talking about wheat. This development put out a whole new spin on things. A new picture of the situation was coming to light, but while the shape was appearing, the edges were still fuzzy. I wondered if what I was considering was really possible, or had I reached the corner of absurd insanity in my mind.

I was about to say something further, when another thought came forward, pushing everything to do with Wiggins, Timothy, or even the beautiful Claire straight out of my head. I froze for a moment, holding the receiver in my hand, thinking hard. It was only after Clare shouted my name over and over again that I came back to my senses. I brought the receiver back to my ear. "Claire darling, I have to run now. Please give the old man my regards."

"But wait, what about your telegram?"

"I think you may have already given me the answer to that. Thank you so much."

"What—"

I put down the receiver, saw that Penelope had fallen asleep, and decided that she would be alright for a few hours. I grabbed my hat and coat and rushed outside. Brooks had been sitting comfortably in the shade, but he jumped to his feet as soon as he saw me, the movement sending his hat tumbling from his head. His hand instinctively reached for his pocket. "What is it? Are you alright?"

I ignored his query about my well-being. "Sheppard said he was going to talk to Harrington. Do you think he's still there now?"

Brooks retrieved his hat from the ground where it had fallen. "I believe so. It takes some time to get a sketch artist over to the safe house, and get a sketch drawn. The odds are good that the inspector may still be there."

"Good." I started towards the parking lot, running more than walking.

"Wait," Brooks called out, running after me. "What's going on?"

I called over my shoulder, "I think I've found a way to find this Ross person. He may be the key to cracking the case."

CHAPTER EIGHT

Brooks drove. I wanted to, but since I didn't know where we were going, prudence dictated that he sit behind the wheel. At least he had a newer car than Sally, one that actually included doors and a ceiling. He drove fast, but I noticed he crept to the edge of the speed limit without breaking it. A true upholder of the law. Still, Brooks didn't waste any time, and within fifteen minutes we were parked in front of a seedy motel on the edge of the Hollywood District.

He escorted me took me to a room on the second floor, and gave a special knock. Within moments Sheppard opened the door. He didn't say anything, he just looked at me and my shadow, before opening the door wider.

When I stepped across the threshold, a glimpse was enough to capture the entire room. Harrington was sitting on one of the two twin beds, with an unknown officer perched in a chair by his side. The officer was holding a sketch pad and pencil— and that's all he was doing, holding them. The pencil wasn't moving, wasn't putting graphite onto paper, wasn't turning a blank sheet into something visual. Perhaps I had come in at the end of the process. Perhaps there was a perfect image of Ross already captured on that sheet of paper, but if so, the artist would be packing up the supplies and getting ready to leave. Since he was still sitting there, I conclude that he was having no luck.

The Inspector was clenching his hands together. If that page was as blank as I suspected, I wanted to rip that sketch-book out of the artist's hands and smash it over Harrington's head, but that was me. If Sheppard was experiencing any such impulses, he managed to keep them to himself.

"Parker's been at it for nearly an hour," he said, "and we're still having trouble getting a sketch. It seems that Harrington doesn't really remember what Ross looks like."

That did not surprise me. Harrington didn't pay attention to anyone other than himself. Sheppard looked toward the pair. The officer wilted just a bit under the inspector's icy gaze, and finally put pencil to paper, to make one, last desperate attempt.

I used the time to scratch an itch that was bothering me. "Did you find out about the costume and the gun?"

"I did, and I still can't believe it. Harrington said he returned them to the prop and costume departments."

"What?" He must have returned the costume after I went searching for it.

"He said he didn't need them anymore."

It was so ingenious it was almost ridiculous. Talk about hiding a murder weapon in plain sight. Too bad Harrington was such an idiot. If he had any brains at all he would turn into a criminal genius. "I assume you have retrieved them both."

"Yes, I sent both the gun and the costume to the FBI laboratory for testing. I should get some results back in the next few days, but I'm fairly confident they will find that it was the gun that killed Montgomery."

"Which isn't exactly news."

"Not at all."

"And the sketch?"

Sheppard only replied with a grunt. We stood there in silence, all three of us staring at Parker as he scribbled on his sketchpad. His hand flew across the paper for several minutes, as he followed Harrington's quiet instructions. In my line of work it was a given that I would be watched by many, many eyes as I focused on my craft, but I knew people who didn't enjoy an audience while they were trying to concentrate. It was especially hard when one of those people staring intently at the back of your neck was your boss. I didn't envy Parker at this moment.

He finally put his pencil down. "This is the best I can do."

He handed the sketchpad to Sheppard, before turning his back on us to open a little black case. As he put his supplies away, Sheppard and I inspected the masterpiece. It did show us the face of the man, but that was all. The features were so average, and the image so vague, it could have been anyone off the street. No progress there. Time to try something else. Time to see if my great idea was going to work.

"Forget what Ross looks like. Did Harrington tell you how he got in touch with this mysterious casting director?"

The inspector removed his notebook from his pocket and flipped through the pages. "Apparently Ross gave Harrington a phone number to call in case of an emergency. We checked and found out that it belongs to a standard answering service."

"Is that the type of place where a client calls them later to retrieve their messages?"

"Exactly," Sheppard said. "It's all very efficient, and all very impersonal. No one at the service ever saw Ross in person, all their contact was over the phone. He left no address, and no phone number of his own where he could be reached. Dead end."

"Maybe not."

I approached Harrington who tilted his chin up so he could look down his nose at me. "Oh," he said. "It's you."

Ah, a new member of my fan club. "Yes it's me, and I have a question."

"I don't have to answer to you."

Sheppard moved forward, pulling his coat jacket back just a bit to reveal his gun and badge. "I say you have to answer to him."

Harrington looked at the gun, then up at Sheppard, and pushed his lips together to cover the teeth that must've been grinding. "What do you want to know?"

"Back at the studio you said Mr. Ross was going to give you more scenes so you could solve Montgomery's fake murder, is that right?"

Harrington nodded. "I was to call him after I pretended to kill Mr. Montgomery. Then he would give me new script pages. While I don't exactly know how the scene was envisioned, it was my understanding that it would be revealed that I, as the Masked Avenger, was actually the champion of justice who was removing a wanton criminal, from society."

"The criminal was played by Mr. Montgomery?"

Harrington nodded. "When all the loose ends were nearly tied up in a big bow, Mr. Montgomery would return from the dead, and the new film series would be launched."

"But you didn't call Ross then," Sheppard said catching on.

"No. When I was given the part on the *Case Files* set I decided it didn't really matter to me if we solved Montgomery's fake murder for the press or not, so I didn't follow through."

"But you could still get a hold of Ross if you wanted to," I said. "You could get those script pages from him?"

"I suppose, but why in the world would I? As I said, I have another part."

Sheppard leaned forward. His nose was only inches from Harrington's face. "You will because I'm saying you will."

Harrington reared back. "Okay." Was that a squeak? "What do you want me to say?"

"We want you to call Ross and set up a meeting with him," I said. "Tell him you have been reading about Montgomery's murder and you think it's high time to finish off the scene."

"But I don't need—"

"Lie!" God, this man was difficult.

"But what if he doesn't want to come?"

"Tell him you're having doubts that Montgomery's murder is a fake. He'll come."

"But I can't lie in front of Ross. I don't know how to act like that."

Sure, now he admits he can't act. No matter. "Don't worry about that. You're not the one who's going to be meeting him."

Sheppard stood up straight and stared at me.

"Yes Inspector, I have a plan." I didn't know if it was a good plan, but at least I had one.

***

It was interesting how someone could be walking down the street next to you, but be miles away emotionally. A cold shoulder my ass.

"I don't know why you're so upset, my darling." I pitched my voice high, and kept my tone stringent. "Miss Sally Kahili

Jones, you are so fortunate to have been chosen to spend time in my presence. Millions of girls fight for the opportunity, yet you are the victor. Bask in the glow."

I hauled out a pocket mirror ostentatiously to check my own looks, but I tilted it a little to the right to see part of her profile. Did I just catch the hint of a smile? I piled it on. "I am the greatest human being ever born. World leaders, celebrities, should all lie down before my feet, and you my dear actually have permission to lay your fingers upon my grand forearm—ow." Her fingers pressed deeply into said, grand forearm, derailing my little speech. "Not so tight."

The fingers didn't relax by even a fraction. "It's not funny, Teddy. This masquerade could get you killed."

I wanted to tell her she was exaggerating. I wanted to tell her everything was going to be fine. I tried once, on the eve before I went to war. False assurances didn't work back then, they wouldn't work now. "Well, it is kind of the idea."

Harrington had called and left a message with the service, and we'd waited impatiently for an hour or so, and finally the hotel phone rang. Harrington's hand had shaken a little as he'd answered, but he said all the right things, mainly because I wrote down lines for him on a piece of paper, and he read them into the phone transmitter, while Sheppard and I listened in. Ross said little and I wondered if he'd been surprised that Harrington was still alive. If he was, he'd covered it up quickly, and had agreed to meet the actor at a small café down the street from the studio at two o'clock this afternoon.

I wasn't surprised that he'd agreed so easily to appear. Ross could have disappeared following Montgomery's murder and probably would have never been caught, but he hadn't left. He'd tried to kill me, and he'd tried to kill Harrington. He could never fully relax while we still breathed, so we had to be dealt with. He would try again to kill us both. It wasn't smart, it wasn't prudent, but it was instinctive, and our mysterious Mr. Ross only seemed to be operating on instinct at this point. It was a weakness I was going to exploit. Waiting was not an option. Ross had to be stopped, and my overactive imagination had come up with a plan.

I had been studying Harrington for days, weeks really. Harrington believed he was the most handsome man on the planet, but when you looked closely, we weren't so different. We had the same basic bone structure, and were around the same height and weight. Superficial changes in hair color, nose and brow features, including a scar over the left brow, and a pocket mirror close at hand, and suddenly Teddy Wainwright was gone and the mighty Harrington stood in his place, walking to the café with Sally Jones on his arm.

"I still don't understand why you're the one putting yourself in harm's way," she said.

"Sally, you've met Harrington, have you not?"

"Your point?"

"This could turn into a volatile situation. I'm meeting Ross in a public place. If something happens I'm going to have to react quickly to make sure no one gets hurt. Harrington would turn tail at the first sign of trouble, and the hell with anyone else. So, you see why I had to take his place, don't you?"

"I suppose, but I do wish you'd let me go into the coffee shop with you."

I tried to contain my sigh. She had broached the suggestion for at least a hundred times, and while part of me would've liked to have her support in case of trouble, most of me wanted to keep her safe.

"We've been all through this. It's too dangerous. You're just to be my escort to the restaurant in case our fellow is watching. After we arrive, you are to kiss my cheek, then head off toward the nearest boutique."

"If it's too dangerous for me, it's too dangerous for you. I can handle myself, you know." She could indeed. Her father had made sure of that.

"Normally, I would love to have you by my side in order to protect me," I assured her. "However, as you well know, most American women do not hold a black belt in judo, especially the little twits who Harrington dates. We must act normally, if we're not to scare off our prey."

"I suppose," Sally conceded.

"I shall be fine. Inspector Sheppard will be waiting in a car across the street, and he assures me that he will have a man inside the coffee shop. A man who was only assigned this case this morning, so he shouldn't be recognized as a police officer."

"Even with his presence, I won't stop worrying until this is all over."

Neither would I. "All will go well," I assured her, "and hopefully it will end with Mr. Ross safely behind bars."

"I hope so."

We approached the restaurant, successfully maintaining our pose as an ordinary couple. Once in the doorway, I handed Sally five dollars, kissed her on the cheek, and sent her on her way. Then I gathered my courage and stepped inside.

It was, I suppose, a perfect example of a typical coffee shop. Booths on one side, a counter and stools on the other. A giant mirror filled the wall opposite the counter, giving the wide angle image of the rest of the shop. Red and white checkered cloths covered the tables. Placed on top of the checks were menus, silverware and vases full of flowers.

I forced myself to not look around as I walked toward a

booth in the rear. I didn't see anyone out of the corner of my eye who looked like a cop, but I was hoping Sheppard's man was there all the same. I settled into a chair, making sure to sit facing the door. After I gave the waitress my order for coffee, I slid out the small mirror from my pocket and started to preen.

The mirror was Harrington's; he carried in a breast pocket over his heart. I wanted an authentic prop for my little play. It was such a little thing, a pocket mirror, but you would have thought we were stealing the Hope Diamond from the fuss he put up. Then Sheppard offered to trade the mirror for a set of handcuffs. It seemed, for a second, that jail was more preferable to Harrington than giving up his precious looking glass, but he reluctantly chose freedom, if one could call staying in that seedy hotel freedom, and handed over the mirror.

Now, sitting in the coffee shop booth, the mirror was coming in handy. If anyone cared to glance my way, they would see that I appeared to be only interested in myself. I was putting on a good act, the act of a self-conscious man, but I was able to turn my major prop into an advantage. If I tilted the mirror a certain way, I could see the reflection off of the big mirror over the counter, therefore allowing me to see the front door and most of the coffee shop, without looking suspicious.

I started my surreptitious search, but none of the people in the restaurant seemed to match Harrington's vague description of Ross. One young man sat at the counter, enjoying a piece of pie. Hopefully he was Sheppard's man. There were three construction workers on their lunch break, and a young couple in the corner exchanging adoring glances over ice cream sodas. Ah, young love. Still, there was no sign of my prey.

I was beginning to worry that this effort would be all for

naught when an older man shuffled through the front door. I held the mirror steady, while supressing a sudden rush of adrenaline. He was the closest thing to Ross to enter the shop yet.

I pretended not to notice him until he settled down in the seat across from me, and then I carefully put the mirror away. Ross turned out to be a middle-aged man with gray hair, slightly balding on top. He had bushy gray eyebrows and a salt-and-pepper mustache and beard. He wore a plain brown suit, and clutched a brown fedora between his hands.

Everything about him was plain. It was as if he was making every effort possible not to stand out. The only color on him at all was some red ink stains on his fingers. He said nothing.

I didn't want him to study me for too long in case he saw through my disguise, so I jumped into the conversational pool first. "Thank you so much for coming, Mr. Ross." I tried my best to match Harrington's high-pitched whine, and thought it was pretty close. "Some silly accident has put shooting of the *Case Files* movie on hold, so while I was waiting I was thinking we could finish off the Montgomery scenes. The paper still says he's been murdered. Don't you think it's time for him to come back from the dead?"

I was baiting him a little, taking a risk, but if we were going to stop him, risks had to be taken.

Ross didn't overtly react. He seemed to be a man in complete control. "Perhaps," he said. "First I want to talk to you about that 'silly' accident. Are you alright?"

"Oh, that." I, or should I say Harrington, waved that away. "Some prop man got some bottles mixed up. It was nothing really."

"I'm pleased to hear it." Ross didn't seem so pleased at all. He looked angry and I knew darn well why. He wanted

Harrington dead, and now he was going to have to find some other way to make that happen. "And you are quite right of course. I agree it is time to settle this Montgomery matter, once and for all."

I perked up like a good little Harrington. "That's fantastic, Mr. Ross. Once Mr. Montgomery introduces me as RKM Studios' newest detective character the public will fall in love. They have been denied access to my talents for far too long."

"Yes they have." A grim little smile came to Ross' lips. One which contained no mirth or joy whatsoever. "I have the script pages back at my apartment. If you will come with me, we will finish this last act today."

"Of course." I was hoping the act would play out differently. I took my time getting to my feet, giving Sheppard's man time to see we were on the move. This was, of course, assuming Sheppard's man was indeed there, and was indeed paying attention. Otherwise, I was heading for a one-way trip.

But with each step toward the front door, my confidence grew. I had done it. The killer walked beside me, accepting my impersonation of Harrington. I had been able to use my dramatic skills to draw a killer out of the woodwork. It hadn't been the first time I'd done this, but I was pleased to see that I still had the knack. The streets of Hollywood would soon be safer, thanks to me. I really was the greatest actor which ever lived.

Whoa. I was living the part a little too well if I was beginning to think like Harrington. When I got home, I was going to take a long, hot shower. Hopefully I could wash away Harrington's conceit along with his hair color. If I survived long enough to get home.

Once I got Ross out of the coffee shop, Sheppard could easily get his hands on this guy and arrest him. I was sure the inspector would be able to extract a confession easily once Ross was safely incarcerated. Everything was working out just fine. Just a few more steps until we were at the front door and this would all be over—"

"Oh, Mr. Wainwright."

Oh no.

Trudy Grainger rushed through the front door of the café, autograph book clutched in her hand. Billy, the ever-silent boyfriend, walked in quietly behind her.

She ran right up to me and pushed the book against my chest. "Mr. Wainwright. I totally forgot that I promised to get your autographs for my friends Nancy, Dougie, and Janet."

Oh, God. She called me Wainwright.

Next to me, I heard a rustle of fabric. The sound clothes made when a man was shifting his limbs. Ross was tense. My disguise was a disguise no more.

Trudy gushed on; oblivious to the danger she was in. "I happened to be watching when you left your bungalow in this silly disguise. Are you practicing for a new part? Anyway, it was a challenge following you. Billy almost lost you on Sunset, still, here we are."

Yes, here they were, ruining everything. I glanced at Ross. The joyless smile was gone. His lips were pulled tight as a drum, and his cheeks had reddened. Dammit. Anger in a killer was not a good thing. The situation was rapidly spiraling out of control. We had seconds before Ross would act and innocent people would die. I had to do something.

Wait. Was that a bit of spirit gum I saw on the edge of his beard? If Ross was wearing a disguise, maybe he was an actor, or some sort of a veteran of the stage.

The barrel of a pistol emerged from Ross' pocket. It

arched up toward me, with the annoying, yet innocent Trudy Granger in between myself in the bullet.

"Look out!"

I grabbed hold of Trudy, ignoring her squeal of delight as her idol actually laid hands on her, and pulled her to the floor. I covered her with my body, muscles in my back tensing up, expecting the impact of bullets any second. While I waited for death, gunshots ripped through the air, followed by screams, shouts, and girly giggles. Trudy, of course. More shouts, the sound of breaking glass, and running feet.

Finally, there was silence. I lay there for a few minutes, just savoring the fact that I was still alive, when a voice came from below. "Why Mr. Wainwright. I do believe you're being fresh with me."

I opened my eyes and found Trudy's lips inches away from mine.

"Gah." I leapt to my feet, backing away to a safe distance. Trudy remained where she had fallen. For a moment, I was afraid she'd been hit by a stray bullet, but her face burst into a broad smile. She'd enjoyed the feeling of my body pressed up against hers, way more than I did, but that was alright, as long as she wasn't hurt.

Was anyone else? I looked around what was left of the coffee shop, and thought I had been transported back into a war zone. It seemed like every glass and bottle in the place was broken. The mirror over the bar was in a shambles. Somebody was going to experience a lot of bad luck in the next few years. I hoped it was Ross. Tables were overturned, chairs broken. Women were crying, being consoled by their men, some of whom looked like they wanted to cry too.

Despite the upheaval, I found no trace of blood and no sign of serious injury. Everyone had been just shaken up by the fracas, but no one had really been injured. There was no sign of Ross, but the ever-so quiet Billy, was bravely helping Trudy to her feet. Confident she was in good hands, I gingerly resumed my journey toward the front door.

Sheppard stepped through just as I reached it. The inspector regarded me with a critical eye. "Are you alright?"

"Fine."

Why was he looking so worried? I wasn't hit. I caught a glance of myself in what was left of the mirror. My hair was a mess, my putty nose had been ripped away, and half of my plastic scar was dangling over my brow. Right now I was half Harrington and half Wainwright, and neither looked good.

I patted my pocket and found that Harrington's precious mirror was missing. He wasn't going to be happy, and I had a feeling I wouldn't be happy to hear the answer to the one question burning in my mind. "What about Ross? Did you get him?"

Sheppard shook his head. "He got away in the hubbub. I called in his description to headquarters. They will pass it on to every patrolman when he checks in. Everyone will be on the lookout."

"A description may not help much."

"Why not?"

"I noticed some spirit gum around the beard on Ross' face."

"So, the beard was a phony?"

I nodded. "He was wearing a disguise, one probably sitting inside a garbage can right now."

"You did think Ross was connected to show business."

"A useless fact."

"True." The inspector patted me on the shoulder. "Don't look so glum. We still have last chance."

"What's that?"

"Maybe I'll catch him when he comes to murder you."

"Comforting, thanks."

While I knew Sheppard was partially kidding, much of what he said was right. Perhaps my murder might be the only way to catch this killer.

CHAPTER NINE

"Teddy."

Why can't real life be more like the movies, I thought while I stroked Penelope's back. She arched slightly, her fur silky smooth beneath my fingers, before she nestled more comfortably on my lap.

"Teddy, you're not listening to me."

Here we'd tracked down a killer, seemingly from nowhere, and now due to the innocent actions of a young girl, he had gotten away. Perhaps for good.

"Teddy."

Why couldn't Ross be safely behind bars now, and who the hell was he really? Damn it. There always was a satisfactory unmasking of the criminal in the *Detective Tompkins* stories by now, so where was my happy ending?

"Teddy!"

The shout close to my ear sent a piercing shockwave directly to my brain. I jerked in my seat, nearly throwing Penelope to the floor. She held on, thanks to twenty claws piercing through the cloth of my trousers, some catching onto my skin below, all digging in so she could maintain her position on my lap. I forced the muscles in my legs to relax, thereby allowing Penelope to relax her painful death grip as well.

When the pain receded enough so I could think clearly again, I looked up to find Sally standing just inches away from me with a rolled up script in her hand. A script that could double for a club if she put her mind to it, and it seemed like she might be inclined to do exactly that.

Time to make nice. "Hello beautiful. I'm sorry, I didn't hear you walk up."

"Obviously. I've been trying to get your attention for a couple of minutes. I need to give you these changes."

She started to throw the script in my lap, but it was only her consideration for my cat that stopped her at the last second. Instead she carefully handed the pages over, and I accepted it like a treasure it was. I flipped through the pages of the script. They were awash with passages, rewritten in red. "Farnsworth sticking his nose into your writing again?"

"I think he must have a gallon of red ink in his basement," Sally sighed." He's constantly making changes with that fountain pen of his. I keep expecting him to run out of ink, but he never does."

"Hmm," I answered. Farnsworth foibles didn't really stack up against the hunt for a murderer.

"Teddy!"

Sally's sharp command snapped my attention back toward her once again. "Yes?"

She stared at me, her eyes hard and her expression tight. After a minute or so, the coldness faded away, and was replaced with a look far more caring. "You don't have to worry, Teddy. I'm sure Brooks will be able to keep you safe until the inspector catches Ross."

I glanced over to the corner where Brooks was sitting in a director's chair, watching everything going on around us. "I know he will. Brooks is a good man."

"Yes he is." Sally gave me that special look of hers. The one that said I had no secrets from her. "But you're not worried about your own safety, are you?"

I shook my head.

Sally appropriated an extra chair and sat down next to me. She took my hand into hers, careful not to nudge Penelope, who had fallen back asleep. "What's really bothering you, Teddy?"

"I'm missing something. I keep having the feeling that I know something, or I've learned something that would help me catch this fellow, but darned if I know what it is."

"The more you think about it, the more it slips away?"

"Exactly."

"Perhaps you're trying too hard," she patted my hand. "Think about something else for a while. Maybe it will come to you."

Sally was an expert in many things, but being subtle wasn't one of them. "You want me to concentrate on my work, don't you?"

"You have at least a dozen new lines to memorize, and you step in front of the cameras in just fifteen minutes."

"You're right, as always."

I passed Penelope over into Sally's care, and got back to work. I tried to memorize my new lines as quickly as I could. It wasn't hard, just incredibly annoying. Most of the changes in the dialogue replaced perfectly fine words with the least objectionable—which you could interpret to mean bland and boring—alternative available. Drat it. The *Detective Tompkins Mysteries* would never be considered the kind of high art to win an Academy Award or some such thing, but they were entertaining, at least until today. Changes like these did not bode well for the future of motion pictures, but there was nothing to be done about it now. I would do the best I could, carry on, and try to fight this fight another day.

My director, Douglas Keene, called for me from across the room. Douglas got his start in directing during the silent era of filmmaking, but when the talkies came around, we discovered that we got along fabulously. Our partnership in creating the *Detective Tompkins Mysteries* had been a long and profitable one. He was by nature a quiet man, sometimes as quiet as the silent films he originally directed. So when he spoke up, I always knew it would be for matters of import, and it would be to my benefit to listen to him carefully.

It was no different this time. I went across the room and received some last minute instructions for today's filming. As usual, we were filming one of the last scenes in the *Detective Tompkins and the Case of the Two-Faced Woman* picture first: the one where Detective Tompkins unmasked the killer. All the usual suspects were gathered around, and the scene could've been really boring. Just a bunch of people sitting in a room. But Douglas was trying some unique things. Usually scenes like this one were filmed in one wide shot, with only a couple of close-ups edited in. People were generally frozen in place, either sitting or standing while they listened to the mighty detective unmask the killer. Because of restrictions with cameras and lighting, there was very little physical movement in scenes like these. Until now. Douglas told me he was going to try some different camera angles where Detective Tompkins could actually walk back and forth across the set. It was innovative and exciting and I couldn't wait to try it.

We set up an immediate rehearsal. While I was walking

back and forth along the set, trying to memorize the places I would step and the places I would stand, I stumbled. Douglas asked me if I was alright, and I assured him I was, but I wasn't really paying attention to him. I really wasn't paying attention to anything in the real world at that moment.

I had it. What had been nibbling at the back of my mind for days had burst forth into my conscious, whole and complete.

I knew who the murderer was.

I wanted to stop pacing and start dancing. I had been fighting with this puzzle for days, and now it was solved. I had positioned the clues I had acquired along the way into the proper order, so that I finally had the whole picture. The right thing to do would be to hand the killer over to Brooks and be done with it. That was what a good little citizen would do and I was a good little citizen, wasn't I?

Apparently I wasn't. An impulse came out of nowhere and shocked the hell out of me. I didn't want to just hand over the killer, I wanted to unmask him, just like Detective Tompkins, in a room full of all the suspects. I wanted to, just once, take a scene from the movies and let it play out in real life. But I certainly didn't want a killer to go free while I indulged an impulse.

I had no proof this man was guilty. I had to get something solid on this man, and the best way to do that would be in true Detective Tompkins fashion: by gathering all the suspects together and maneuvering the situation so the guilty party would reveal his own guilt.

I told Douglas that I thought I had the positioning down, and requested a small break. I returned to Sally and Penelope and snatched up a small notebook, and started scribbling. Once I was done I glanced at Brooks, who casually walked over. I whispered a few urgent requests in his ear, then ripped a page from the notebook and handed it to him. Placing his hat on his head, he nodded and headed out the door.

"What was that all about?" Sally asked me.

"He's gone to gather all the suspects."

"What?"

Her voice was just a tad too loud, the kind of volume that attracted attention, so I politely shushed her. "You'll see, and very soon. I beg of you to be patient."

"I am always patient with you, Teddy," she whispered, "but I swear I will twist your legs and arms into a pretzel if you don't tell me what's going on."

"There's no time. We're going to shoot in a few minutes and I have to make sure I memorize the script changes."

She couldn't argue with that since she was the one who wanted me to memorize the changes in the first place, but I could tell she wasn't mollified. Hopefully she would be soon. Hopefully we all would be soon.

I studied the script for a few moments, and Douglas called for everyone to take their places. He was ready to film. But I wasn't ready, Brooks wasn't back yet, and I couldn't stall. I had to carry on as usual until they arrived. I got up from my chair I stepped before the cameras.

A man came through the small door leading toward the outside world and stood at the far side of the set. It was Farnsworth. He was on the list of names I handed to Brooks, but since the police officer had not yet returned with the others, it seemed the Paragon of Virtue had decided to grace me with a visit all by himself. Although at the moment it would have been more accurate to call Farnsworth the Paragon of Disapproval, judging by the sour twist of his lips. How anyone could go through life so unhappy all the time was beyond me. You could find no joy within if you spent all your time finding fault with others.

I wondered what sparked the personal visit, but really had no time to dwell on such things. We were ready to shoot. I took my time to find my mark, and was glad I did. The person-size door opened up once again, and in came Inspector Sheppard with a group of people. Douglas turned around, saw the group, and was about to say something when I spoke up. "It's okay Douglas, they are some guests that I have invited to watch today's filming."

Douglas studied me in that usual quiet way of his. Never before had I invited guests to be on our soundstage when we were working. Even more out of the ordinary was the selection of people who had come to visit. In addition to the inspector and Brooks, there was Timothy, Mr. Owens, Harry the prop master, and wonders of wonders, the great Lance Hudson. No wonder Douglas was confused. Lance never lowered himself to set foot upon a set other than his own. The visit was breaking a shocking precedent, one of which the great actor would never have consented to do freely. I noticed Brooks was standing close to Lance with his hand inches from the great one's arm. I wonder if Brooks actually had to twist it in order to get Lance to come, but it wasn't important. They were all here, which was all that mattered. Brooks looked toward Farnsworth, then me, and nodded. It was time to begin.

I walked over to the director's chair. "Thank you for indulging my little whim to have guests today Douglas, I really appreciate it."

"It's my pleasure, Teddy," Douglas said slowly, aware that something strange was going on. I leaned forward to give him a friendly pat on the shoulder, and urgently whispered in his ear. "No matter what happens in the next few minutes Douglas, keep filming. Don't stop."

Douglas stiffened, but that was his only reaction to my request. The director pulled away from me and began shouting orders.

The other actors and I took our places on the set, and Douglas called for action. I immediately assumed the mantle of the detective and started to solve the case, beginning with the fictional crime. "One of you killed the Prince of Parnasia." I made a point to sweep my eyes across the assembled actors in the scene as I read my lines, enjoying the freedom to walk as I spoke. Such a novelty. "I was unable to make any progress in uncovering the killer's identity, until I uncovered his motive. The key is a small baby left on the front steps of an orphanage many years ago. A baby who was the illegitimate child of—"

"Stop!" The voice came from my right. Although unexpected, the Paragon of Virtue was making himself heard. Farnsworth ignored the cry of dismay from Douglas and the groans from the crew around him. He shoved everyone in his way as he marched up to me and waved a script in my face. "You idiot! You can't mention an illegitimate child on film," he spat. "Didn't you read the changes?"

"Yes sir." I took a deep breath, and drew upon the best of my acting skills to project an aura of calm. "I'm so sorry, Mr. Farnsworth, you are quite correct. I simply lost my place for a moment." My unabashed apology seemed to catch the censor off guard. He'd probably been expecting some sort of argument. "Please allow me to try again."

"Very well." Farnsworth returned to his original position. "Just make sure you get it right this time."

"Yes sir." I looked around to my crew. "Sorry about that."

The crew returned to their stations, ready to begin once again. Everyone was in place now. It was time to really begin the final scene of this drama.

An assistant came forward with a clap board. "*Detective Tompkins and the Case of the Two Faced Woman,*" he shouted. "Scene forty-one. Take two." The clap board snapped together, followed by the shout of action from Douglas.

Once again, all eyes were on me. "Ladies and gentlemen. I have gathered you all here in the hopes of identifying a killer, but in order to do so, I must take you all back to the night of the murder." I started to pace, just a detective on the job, but ever mindful of the camera. I took care to stay along the path that Douglas had sketched out for me earlier. "This was the most ingenious of killings, thought out by the most clever of villains. It wasn't a crime of passion." I was warming up to my topic. "No, this was the most thought-out and diabolical murder ever imagined, because this killer found himself the most unique of weapons to kill his victim. Another human being."

That was definitely off script, but this time Farnsworth didn't let out a peep. The other actors had lines, but they seemed to be caught up in my narrative, and didn't say a word. I shot a glance toward Timothy, who was observing the proceedings with interest. Harry studied the props on the set, like any prop man would. I saw that Lance had commandeered a chair, and was leaning back with his arms crossed, occasionally glancing at his watch. In contrast to his relaxed air, Sheppard and Brooks stood straight and ready, hands near their coat pockets. I hoped there were real guns in those pockets, ready to be used if need be.

With the comforting sound of the camera, still rolling in the background, I continued on. "Using a clever wit, and taking advantage of one man's vanity, our killer was able to get another man to do his dirty work for him, all while convincing his hapless tool that he hadn't committed a murder at all. Brilliant." No one was moving. I feared some weren't even breathing. "But who was the mastermind behind this ingenious crime, and why did he want our victim dead? The question continued to evade me. Even after a threat and an attempt on my life motivated me into further investigation, the answers eluded me. Was it the script girl who was doing all the work, while her boss took all the credit?" I risked a glance Sally's way. She took Penelope from her lap and settled my princess on my director's chair. Perhaps she was getting ready to smack me when I got off the set. That would be alright. I knew she would forgive me later. "Was it the casting director, whose decisions were constantly being overruled?" Timothy straightened just a little, knowing I was talking about him. Where his lips curling into a smile? I moved on. "Was it the prop man who replaced a fake sugar bottle with a real one, with the intent of massive bodily harm?" Harry was no longer staring at the props. He was staring at me. "Or was it the actor who was forced to share the silver screen with an idiot who had no talent and whose presence would ruin his film?" Lance uncrossed his arms.

Everyone on the set seemed to be frozen in place. It was now perfectly clear that I was no longer acting, but actually talking about real people. "It certainly wasn't the idiot who pulled the trigger, but in order to get his plot to work, our killer knew his way around a studio. He had access to wardrobe, makeup, and personnel."

The still-rolling camera whirred as I paced closer to the edge of the set. "I came across several clues in my investigation, but none of them made sense. They were a collection of random facts, bouncing around in my mind, until now." Abandoning all pretense, I left the set altogether, the camera faithfully following my every move. I went to my canvas chair and picked up my script. "This turned out to be the key."

"But that's just an ordinary screenplay, isn't it?" Timothy asked.

"No, Timothy, this script is far from ordinary," I walked to the rear of the sound stage. "In fact, it's the key to the case. Do you know why Mr. Farnsworth?"

As I stood in front of him, the Paragon of Virtue, seemed far from virtuous. His face was red, and his hair was damp with sweat. Farnsworth looked downright scared. "I'm… I'm afraid I don't know what you're talking about," he stammered.

"I don't suppose you do," I agreed. "The clues you left behind we're so subtle, so inconsequential, they went unnoticed by everybody. Even Inspector Sheppard here."

Instead of taking offense, Sheppard took the opportunity to move nearer to Farnsworth. "What clues?" he barked.

"This," I held up the script. "If you look inside you'll see several pages marked up with red ink."

"So?" Farnsworth seemed to finally notice that events were taking a turn not fortunate to him. "It's my job to rewrite copy. There's nothing unusual in that."

"By itself no, I agreed, "but I also found a marked up script inside Harrington's apartment."

"Also not unusual," Farnsworth argued, although his complexion paled just a bit more. "I'm not sure who this Harrington person is, but if any actor works on this lot, it's only natural that he would have several such scripts lying around."

"Ah, here's the rub," I countered. "Harrington said the man who gave him the gun he used to kill Montgomery handed him script pages. A script I looked at later when I was in his hotel room. I didn't realize it at the time, but it was the script that laid out Montgomery's murder on paper. It also had several notations written on it. Notations made with a red pen."

"That still doesn't prove it was me," Farnsworth countered.

"Did this Harrington person identify me as his visitor?"

"No, the man he described looked different," I admitted.

"Well, there you go."

"I believe you were in disguise," I countered. "You used to be an actor. You had skills in makeup. You could have changed your looks easily."

"That doesn't mean I did."

"No," I agreed. "Having a theatrical past is not enough to convict you."

"Then we are done here," Farnsworth said with confidence, and started to walk away.

"Not quite." I didn't shout, but my voice was firm. It was the sound of a man sure of his convictions. Farnsworth stopped in his tracks. "There are more things that identify a man than the features on his face, you know."

Farnsworth stared straight ahead at a blank wall. "Like what?"

"Look at your fingertips."

Farnsworth didn't look, but everyone else in the studio did. They saw red ink stains on his thumbs and index fingers.

I moved forward, and confronted Farnsworth face to face. "When I met with the killer in the coffee shop," I said, "I noticed that red ink stained his fingertips. Red ink stains just like these." I grasped Farnsworth's hand. He didn't flinch at my touch. I raised his hand upwards so the camera could get a better look. Too bad it was filled with black and white film, but I was hoping some streaks of darkness could be seen against his lighter skin. "At first I couldn't understand why a killer would use so much red ink. There were so many stains, and some of them seemed very old. The killer probably used a red pen nearly every day, but why? Then I remembered those marked up pages on the script in Harrington's room."

There was fear in Farnsworth's eyes. I was on the right track. "You couldn't help it, could you? Making changes to Harrington's script. Even though you originally wrote it yourself, you changed your mind when you looked it over just before you gave it to him. Originally you thought you needed to be much more dramatic to convince Harrington to do your bidding, but the Paragon of Virtue was too deep inside you to let such violence it go unchecked. You edited your own work, even if it was going to be instrumental to your plan. You couldn't help it. It was in your nature."

The stage was dead still. No one moved. I wasn't sure if anyone breathed. Farnsworth sure didn't look like he was breathing.

"So, when I saw the red ink on your fingers, I knew you were the killer, but why would you kill Montgomery? Then I realized that virtue was exactly at the heart of the matter, wasn't it, Mr. Farnsworth?" His eyes flicked back-and-forth, searching for a way out. I hurried on. "The Motion Picture Decency Code was forced upon every lot in Hollywood. Every lot except this one. We got away with whatever we wanted for years, while other studios had to adhere strictly to the code. Why?"

Sheppard had the answer. "Blackmail."

"Exactly," I acknowledged. "Thank you, Inspector." I turned back to Farnsworth. "Montgomery must have known something about you. Something you were desperate to keep out of the public eye. Something so dire, you would allow this studio to become a hub of heathen activity for years. Now, I have no idea what information Montgomery had, but since you wish everyone to follow your example of virtuous behavior, I can't help but wonder if you perhaps weren't so virtuous in the past, and Montgomery found out about it." His face flushed. A sign of guilt. I had him. "Is that it, Mr. Farnsworth? You made one mistake in your life, and Montgomery was making you pay for it, reminding you of it every day for years? Did it wear on your soul so much you finally decided committing one murder was less of a sin than allowing R.K. to continue his movie house of moral degradation? Is that when you decided to kill him?"

It was too much for any man to take, even the Paragon of Virtue. Farnsworth snapped. He forgot there was a room full of people watching him, forgot there was a camera recording his every move. He even forgot there were two policemen standing only a few feet away. Farnsworth forgot everything and ran for the door, believing, perhaps because he wished it, he could simply get away.

Oh, he made a good effort. His panic gave him enough strength to push Sheppard into Brooks when the inspector tried to stop him. The men tumbled to the ground. While they fought to untangle their limbs, my heart seemed to stop.

Then he made a huge mistake. He ran right past Sally.

Sally. My dear, sweet, Sally, with a father who was an army judo instructor. As soon as Farnsworth got in range, she planted her feet wide, turned her hand into a make-shift knife and slashed down. Her hand struck the back of his neck, and that was all it took. Within seconds, he was laying on the ground, out cold. She brushed her hands together and smiled the most satisfying smile I had ever seen from her.

Sheppard and the rest of the crew stared at her in shock, and with a little bit of respect. For me, I was just so proud of my Sally, and more than a little relieved. The most important scene of my life was over, and it had turned out alright.

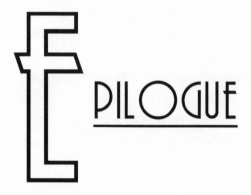

EPILOGUE

I was sitting at an outdoor table in front of the commissary. The edict came down long ago that said Penelope was not welcome inside, and on the days I had her with me, I wasn't welcome inside either, which was fine with me. Despite it being nearly Thanksgiving, it was a warm day in sunny Southern California. The sun, gently beating down, was warm against my skin. With Penelope nestled in my lap, I felt comfortable and relaxed, probably for the first time since I walked into Montgomery's office and found his lifeless body slumped over the desk.

It had taken Farnsworth several minutes to recover from Sally's stunning judo chop, but once he was safely on his feet, Sheppard had cheerfully slapped the cuffs on him and hauled him off to jail. After peace was restored, I'd went back to work and shot the final scene of "*Detective Tompkins and the Two-Faced Woman*" this time following the original script, minus Farnsworth's ridiculous changes.

Sheppard said he was going to need the footage we shot of Farnsworth's attempted escape to use in court, but I was hoping to get it back some day. I wanted to send a copy of Sally's judo move to her dad in Hawaii.

"Who would have ever believed meek and mild Mr. Farnsworth could be capable of such an intricate plot."

I opened my eyes and saw Timothy standing next to me. He had a tray in his hands, complete with two cups of coffee, and a bowl of water for Penelope.

With a smile, I gestured toward the empty chair next to me, and reached for my cup of coffee. "I was expecting you sooner."

The tray jiggled as Timothy placed it on the table. "You were?"

"You know I was."

"I do?"

"Must you make inane comments?" I glanced toward the watch on his wrist. "You know Farnsworth was trying to frame you with a watch like that. He wore it when he attacked me on the road."

"He did?"

I sighed. Timothy should never try to become an actor. He didn't have the knack. "Yes. Farnsworth thought to throw me off the trail by making me suspect you, and it worked for a bit."

Timothy sipped his coffee with one hand, and petted Penelope with the other. "Worked until—"

"Until I learned from the secretary of my former employer, that said employer had gone to a certain gentleman's club in the nation's capital."

"Why is that so unusual? I'm sure people attend gentle-men's clubs all the time."

"Ah, but this is a special club," I said, leaning forward. "It caters to a certain clientele. The type of man who engaged in certain clandestine activities during the last great war."

"Oh really," Timothy said while leaning back comfortably in his chair. "How interesting."

It wasn't really so interesting to one who already knew. "Yes, my former employer went to visit that club right after I cabled him to ask for more information about you."

"Me?" The outrage was a bit forced. "You actually felt the need to check up on me?"

"I must admit it made me a rather bit uncomfortable, but I really didn't know much about you, Timothy, and there was the watch after all."

"Ah yes, the watch. Making me suspect number one I suppose."

"That and the threat."

Timothy sat up straight. I had finally surprised him. "What threat?"

"Oh didn't I tell you," I asked innocently. "I got a letter in the mail that was full of threatening words spelled out with the most atrocious grammar, all in block letters cut out from newspapers and magazines. Warning me off of the case."

"Oh dear, that is unsettling." Timothy leaned back in his chair once again. "What makes you think Farnsworth didn't send it?"

"He could have, and for a while I thought he might have, after he discovered that my interest in Montgomery's murder went beyond my involvement caused by finding the body."

"How did he tumble onto you?"

"I think it was when I lost Harrington's address. It had been in my pocket, then I went to visit Sally in her office. After I had a confrontation with Farnsworth, I discovered it was gone."

"So now Farnsworth knew you were sticking your nose into things where it didn't belong?"

"Indeed. I think he might have even followed me while he was in disguise. There were plenty of downtrodden men in the lobby of Harrington's hotel, and there were plenty of people in front of the police precinct who could have seen me talk to Sheppard. I believe that's when Farnsworth decided I needed to be eliminated."

"By attacking you on the road," Timothy said.

"Exactly." I waited for Timothy to understand the subtext in this scenario, and it didn't take long.

"Ah, I see. Farnsworth wouldn't have written you a threatening note if he had already intended to kill you."

"No he wouldn't. That threat came shortly after I sent my cable to my former employer. A cable inquiring about you."

Timothy leaned forward, his hand on his chest. "And you think I actually had the audacity to send this threat?"

"Oh no, no, no. I know you didn't send it."

"Well if not me, and not Farnsworth, then who?"

"I think it might have come from the person my former employer met with at said gentleman's club in the nation's capital."

"And who might that be?"

"Perhaps a man once in the same line of work as my former employer. Perhaps a former employer of yours."

There it was, aired out in plain sight, even if I didn't plainly say so. Once I got out of the trenches of France, I served my country during the great war in certain, unspecified manner. Perhaps Timothy served his country in a similar manner.

Timothy was looking at me strangely, as if he had never really seen me before. Perhaps he was becoming just as enlightened as I.

I raised my coffee cup toward him. "A toast, to all those who served during the great war, in whatever capacity."

Timothy hesitated for a moment, and then a genuine smile crossed his face. He eagerly clinked his coffee cup against mine. "A fine toast indeed." We drank for a few moments in silence, then Timothy put his cup down. "I am sorry about that letter. I believe whoever sent it must have sent it by mistake. You are obviously no threat to anyone."

"To anyone who's not a killer."

"Agreed." Timothy drained his coffee cup dry. "So Farnsworth tried to frame me, did he?"

"He did. That man certainly was not a Paragon of Virtue. I wonder what information Montgomery was using to blackmail him."

"I can answer that." The mighty Inspector Sheppard tossed his hat on the table, and dropped into an empty chair with a sigh.

"Inspector," I said. "Would you like something to drink?"

"No thanks. I just stopped by to rest my feet a minute, and give you an update on the case."

"Nice of you."

"I suppose it's the least I could do," the inspector said, looking everywhere but at me. "Since you did help in Farnsworth's capture."

Ah, a compliment, and knowing how he felt about celluloid detectives, a big one. "You said you knew something about Farnsworth's motive," I asked, hoping to move us beyond this awkward moment.

"Yes, I did," Sheppard spoke quickly. "He's singing like a canary now, in order to try to reduce his sentence."

"And?" I prompted.

"And it turns out that once upon a time, the Paragon of Virtue had a mistress."

"How interesting. Let me guess. Said mistress, at one time, wanted to be an actress."

"No surprise there really I suppose," Sheppard said. "Farnsworth was apparently in love with the girl. He loved her so much he was willing to go to ask his friend R.K. Montgomery to help him out. Shortly after that the studio head gave her a small part in the chorus of one of those big musical productions."

"Let me take my guess one step further," I put in. "Said affair with said mistress soon petered out. While she was removed from the situation, Montgomery still had knowledge of the affair. If he wanted, Montgomery could not only ruin the reputation of the Paragon of Virtue, but could also drop a word into the ear of Mrs. Farnsworth, which could be just as devastating."

"Exactly."

"That's why Montgomery was so successful in keeping the code off of our lot," I said. "R.K. forced Farnsworth to back off by threatening to tell all."

"Finally, Farnsworth got tired of it, and arranged to remove the giant thorn in his side."

"By conning an egomaniac into committing a murder for him."

"Ingenious," Sheppard said.

"And a little scary," Timothy added.

"Well, as much as I enjoyed this little interlude, crime waits for no man." The police inspector hauled himself to his feet. "Time to escape this la-la land before I get sucked in for good."

"You're welcome here anytime."

Sheppard laughed. "I'd better not be back here soon, you read me?"

In other words, stay out of trouble. After my near miss with the Grim Reaper, it was a command I would be happy to obey. "Yes sir." I gave him a mock salute. He just shook his head and walked away, heading back toward those mean streets outside the studio gates.

I glanced at my watch. I had an hour or so before I was due back on the set, so Timothy graciously let me stay with Penelope while he went inside for refills for our coffee. He didn't return alone. Sally had joined him. She gracefully sat next to me, looking happier than had ever seen her before. "Oh Teddy, did you hear the news?"

"Apparently not." I hadn't heard about anything that could bring her such joy. "What happened?"

"Well I had a little chat with Mr. Owens after Farnsworth was taken away. While Mr. Farnsworth hadn't been doing anything as low as blackmail, I did point out to Mr. Owens that perhaps he shouldn't have acquiesced to Mr. Farnsworth's demands so easily. If Mr. Owens was going to be the new head of the studio, he was going to have to take a firmer grip on things. He asked me if I had anything specific in mind, and I said I did."

I bet she did, but knew better than to say so. "What did you suggest to him?"

"I said that it was high time that the people on this lot who actually do the work get recognized for it. Especially when it came to the writing department."

"Really?" I had no doubt that Sally could get what she wanted if she was determined to go about it, but I had never seen her act so forcefully before. "So what did he say to that?"

"He agreed with me," she said smiling. "He said it was high time that Harvey Spencer be transferred, perhaps to some other department back east. Therefore, a new head writer has been appointed to this lot."

I clasped her gloved hand in mine. "Am I speaking to the new head writer now?"

If anyone's eyes could truly sparkle I was looking at the

ones that would. "You are."

I was quite sure my eyes were sparkling too. "Congratulations love. That is wonderful news."

"It is indeed," Timothy added as we both kissed her on the cheek.

It was wonderful news, but I wondered if Owens agreed to the arrangement more out of fear of Sally's judo skills, as opposed to embracing her writing skills. No matter, if anyone deserved this promotion it was my Sally. The writing department at RKM Studios was in good hands.

Timothy had to leave us, so Sally and I spent the next quarter hour bouncing around story ideas. Should Detective Tompkins investigate his next case in Rio or Rome? Both would be recreated here on back lot, darn it, but at least it was fun to dream. We were discussing the details when Lance marched up to the table.

I forced a smile. Perhaps if I told myself that I liked him often enough, I might soon begin to believe it. "Lance. How lovely to see you."

"Thanks. May I join you?" He sat before we could answer, making the question moot. "Congratulations on solving the Montgomery case. Are you planning to leave the silver screen and start detecting full time?"

"In your dreams," Sally's mutter was too quiet for Lance to hear; at least I hoped it was.

"Sorry, Hudson. I think Inspector Sheppard wouldn't be too happy if I stuck my nose into another case. Best to leave things the way they are for now."

"I see." Lance seemed to be a little disappointed. Was he so eager to get rid of me? "Well, I understand that Mr. Owens was impressed with your skills at disguises and wants to cast you in other roles."

"Really, Teddy?" Sally said. "That's wonderful."

"I turned him down."

"What?"

I surprised them both. "I've had enough of disguises for the time being. I think I'd like to settle down and enjoy just being plain, old Detective Tompkins for a while."

"Wonderful," Lance said through clenched teeth.

Dear Lance. He would never learn how to share. "I think there's enough space on the silver screen for the both of us."

"We shall see."

Yes we would.

Then came a sign that perhaps proved him right.

"Oh my goodness," came a squeal that could only belong to the queen of fan mania. Trudy Grainger had arrived. "There you are."

I stood up, straightened my tie, and turned to accept my fate like a man. "Hello, Trudy," I said, pasting a grin on my face.

To my amazement, she rushed by me like I wasn't there, and ran toward Lance's side. "Oh, Mr. Hudson. I am simply your greatest fan," she gushed. "May I have your autograph?"

Sally and I exchanged glances, before turning our heads in unison to stare at the couple. How quickly the sands of fandom shifted.

Lance looked pleased to receive the attention. "Of course, my dear. Who shall I make it out to?" As he signed, I wondered how long it would be before he too joined me on the bottom of the fan base pile.

No matter. I sat back down, petted Penelope, and watched the pair in action. This was one show I was going to enjoy.